DATE DUE

D1443344

To my YOUNG KING KAI . . .

Continue to light up the world with your smile and mind while never allowing a single soul to deter you from your dreams.

Thank you for saving me in my moments of need.

Your energy is rare. Share it sparingly and wisely. Give in abundance to those who feed your soul.

Be open to growth.

Be steady through adversity. Your circle can either elevate or destroy you.

Change is essential . . . in life and with people.

Focus on yourself . . . first and foremost. Your mental, physical, and emotional well-being are priority. Never take that lightly. You can't pour from an empty cup.

Take care of your mother for life. Like my mother . . . she is your direct source of energy and life. You'll breathe easier in her presence.

Love you more than you know. Daddy always got you . . . just like my father always has my back no matter what.

Never settle. You're too special for that.

—Kai Zen Stroman's father

THE SPIN

ALSO BY
MARCUS STROMAN

The Grip

THE SPIN

BY

MARCUS STROMAN

Aladdin
New York   London   Toronto   Sydney   New Delhi

ALADDIN

An imprint of Simon & Schuster Children's Publishing Division
1230 Avenue of the Americas, New York, New York 10020
First Aladdin hardcover edition July 2023
Text copyright © 2023 by Marcus Stroman
Jacket illustration copyright © 2023 by Setor Fiadzigbey
All rights reserved, including the right of reproduction in whole or in part in any form.
ALADDIN and related logo are registered trademarks of Simon & Schuster, Inc.
For information about special discounts for bulk purchases, please contact
Simon & Schuster Special Sales at 1-866-506-1949 or business@simonandschuster.com.
The Simon & Schuster Speakers Bureau can bring authors to your live event.
For more information or to book an event contact the Simon & Schuster Speakers Bureau
at 1-866-248-3049 or visit our website at www.simonspeakers.com.
Jacket designed by Dan Potash
Interior designed by Mike Rosamilia
The text of this book was set in Athelas.
Manufactured in the United States of America 0523 FFG
2 4 6 8 10 9 7 5 3 1
Library of Congress Control Number 2023932666
ISBN 9781665916172 (hc)
ISBN 9781665916189 (ebook)

Don't take criticism from someone
you wouldn't take advice from.
—Marcus Stroman

CHAPTER 1

BOUNCE, BOUNCE, BOUNCE.

I bounce a basketball down the hall on my way downstairs.

"Marcus!" cries my mother as I round the corner to the kitchen. "Have mercy and stop that inside the house!"

I shoot the ball into a basket that holds shoes by the door.

"Nice shot," says my older sister, Sabria, who is already at the table, dunking French toast into syrup.

I sit down next to her.

"Marcus, that ball bouncing everywhere is echoing through the house," says Mom. "It's kind of early for that noise, okay?"

"It's the sound of a basketball!" I say. "That kind of noise is perfect all day long!"

My mother groans. "I need more coffee first."

Mom pauses to pick up her mug as she makes sandwiches. Now that I'm in middle school, my mother has decided that she shouldn't pack my whole lunch. She makes the main part, like a sandwich or pasta, and I have to put in either a piece of fruit or a vegetable and a dessert. I tried to sneak in an extra bag of cookies once, but she checks my lunch every day. When I stay at my dad's house, his thinking is that it's my lunch and I should just take care of it. He doesn't care if I pack an entire bag of Cheetos and call it a day.

"Okay, schedules for the day," Mom says, looking at her phone as my sister and I shoot each other a look. Mom is always focused on schedules. She has charts all over the place listing each kid's activities, practices, and games, and who's doing drop-off or pickup. Now that my parents are divorced, it's a daily thing to go over who'll be there to shuttle everyone around and where we're staying each night, since we go back and forth between Mom's house and Dad's house. Because both of my parents work and because my sports schedules can get a little wild, we don't do one week at Mom's and then one week at Dad's. We switch around a lot, so it makes everything a little bananas.

Even though it's been a while, I'm still getting used to having two houses and two bedrooms. I still don't like it, but the fact is, my parents are divorced, and nothing is going to change that. I've accepted it, but I still sometimes get really mad that we don't all live together. The worst, to me, is toting a bag between houses, because there are some things I only have one of, like my game-day baseball glove, and I have to cart that around. Once, Sabria totally lost it and screamed, "I live out of a bag, and I don't have a home anymore!"

Mom and Dad freaked a little after that, but they sat us down and explained that we now have two houses and two homes but we're still a part of one family. Which we understand, mostly. But still, if you leave a favorite pair of sneakers at one house, then realize two days later that you want to wear them . . . you're out of luck. That makes me mad.

"Marcus, you have basketball after school," says Mom, reading off her chart. "And Sabria is babysitting next door for the twins. Sabria, you'll take the bus home, then walk over there. Marcus, you will stay for practice. Your dad will pick you up and bring you here since I have to work late. You will both be here for dinner and sleep here tonight." Mom nods at the chart. She seems pleased that today is a relatively easy day. Things can get a little out of hand when both Mom and Dad are working nights, especially if both of us kids also have evening activities.

"Homework all done?" asks Mom, eyeing the two of us. Mom and Dad are both strict about homework. Sometimes Dad will let me do homework while I watch a game, but Mom never does. She believes in concentrating.

"But if I can do homework *and* watch a game, isn't that better?" I sometimes ask. "I'm getting practice at doing two things at once. I mean, that has to be better than sitting here only doing one thing, right?"

"No," Mom will say. "There are some things that should have your full attention. Do you want me to drive and make dinner? That would cause a major accident. I'd either crash the car or burn down the house."

I roll my eyes. "That's a fairly crazy example, Mom," I say.

"Would Dad let you break your concentration with baseball practice to play a video game at the same time?" she asks.

I actually laugh at the thought of that. Dad is hard-core about baseball training. Dad is hard-core about a lot of things, but *really* hard-core about my baseball training. Every morning, I practice with Dad, doing drills, throwing, and doing exercises to keep me strong and nimble. If I even try to chat with Dad during practice, he'll rumble back at me.

Thankfully, I did my homework last night. I'm good about doing it, even if I don't always like it or if I'm pretty tired after a game or a practice. The truth? I don't mind school. I like learning new stuff and challenging myself. But most kids don't go around saying that they love school. I might complain about homework, but I always do it. I'm competitive in all things—on courts, on fields, and in classrooms.

Sabria gives me some side-eye. "You know you have a project coming up," she says.

I scowl back since Sabria is always stepping in my business. "I do," I say. "But we haven't even started on it in class. How did you know?"

"I heard you talking about it," says Sabria.

I give her a look. Somehow Sabria manages to "overhear" a lot of stuff. I'm about to accuse her of reading my texts when my mother says, "Marcus, what's the project about?"

"We aren't even supposed to start it yet," I say again, a little huffy. "Don't worry, Mom. I know, I know, school is important."

"It is," says Mom evenly. "But I'm also interested in what you're working on."

"It's for media studies," I say. "It's about why you need multiple news sources to fully understand something. And how you have to look at all the information and then make an informed conclusion for yourself."

"It was boring when we did that unit," says Sabria. Ah, so maybe she wasn't eavesdropping. Maybe she just remembers taking the same class.

"It doesn't sound boring at all!" says Mom. "And it's a very important skill to have. You need to understand what you're reading and understand how you're getting information!"

I smirk at my sister as I slurp down my French toast. Older sisters who always have to be right can be so annoying.

"Okay, let's go, kids," says Mom, glancing at the clock.

Mom or Dad drives us to school instead of making us take the bus, which is fine with me because standing outside at a bus stop does not seem fun, even in perfect weather. Sabria goes to high school, which she thinks is totally cool. It is, but she always complains about how much homework she has, so I'm in no rush to get there.

Dad likes to be focused in the morning, checking in on the news and what our goals are for the day. Mom is a lot more chatty, which can be good, but sometimes I just like it quiet.

We gather up our backpacks and lunches and head toward the car. Sabria gets to the front seat first. I shrug and throw my bag into the back and slide in. If I'm in the back seat, I can kind of just tune everything out, and this morning I'm tired. I already had my daily baseball practice with Dad, and my arm is a little sore. Plus, Dad has me working on core strength and lifting weights. I do a lot even before school starts in the morning.

My dad and I practice every single morning, in the rain, in the cold, even in the snow. No weekends off. Dad thinks I have real talent for baseball and if I work hard and practice, I have a shot at being a pro player. While that sounds kind of cool, the truth is, I'm not totally sure I want to be a professional baseball player. For practically my entire life everyone has said, "Wow, that kid can play" when I'm on the baseball field. It's not that I don't like baseball; I love baseball. But I don't like people deciding things for me. I want some choices, and if I feel like I can work hard and be great at more than baseball, why wouldn't I at least try?

I also love basketball. It's an awesome game, and I practice hard and am pretty decent on the court. I don't feel the same pressure with basketball, because there isn't this expectation of, *Oh, here comes Marcus Stroman. He's supposed to be the best basketball player.* No one says that. And that's cool. It makes me want to be a better basketball player. Maybe I can be a professional basketball player, even if everyone always tells me I'm not tall enough to play.

I must be more zoned out than I realized,

because the sound of the car door slamming startles me. I watch Sabria walking up the path to her school as my mother's gaze follows her. Mom always waits until we're at the door to the school, which makes me half smile and half roll my eyes. Mom isn't afraid we won't actually go in. She just likes to see us get to the door. Mom watches Sabria pull open the main door to the school, then slowly leaves the drop-off lane, glancing at me in the rearview mirror.

As I sit in the car, I'm doing this new thing Gary taught me. Gary is my mental-health coach. A mental-health coach is like a coach for your head, the inside part. Gary helps me process how I feel about things and is helping me see how I react to them too. Sometimes I get really tense or nervous, and Gary shows me how to relax and feel a little looser. It's important in life, but it's also important on the field or the court, when sometimes I really tense up, and as my dad says, I get stuck in my head.

When my dad used to say I was stuck inside my

head, I always had an image of myself literally stuck inside my head, crawling on my hands and knees. It was kind of funny, but it isn't funny at all when things really rattle you.

Gary taught me this game I can use when I get really upset or stressed or stuck. It's called the Senses game because you use all five senses, and, yes, we laugh because it sounds like a game you'd play in preschool, but it really works. You have to look around you and find five things to see, four things to hear, three things to smell, two things to feel, and one thing that would taste good. Sometimes Gary shuffles them around so it's five things to smell or four things to feel. It makes you look around to see where you are and take it in.

If I'm stressed at a baseball game, I can smell the grass, feel the sun, hear crowds chanting (or booing). The cool thing is that while you're doing it, you really notice things you might not normally notice. Once, I had to name five things I smelled at a baseball game, and I realized how much I could smell beyond grass. At one game

I smelled the newly cut grass, sure, but I also smelled hot dogs grilling in the park behind the field, the dirt, sweat (gross but true), and I swore I smelled cologne. For a while after that I wondered which teammate had been wearing cologne to a game.

To be honest, I sometimes do the Senses game when I'm just hanging out, like a mind puzzle. It grounds me.

My school is just down the street from Sabria's, so Mom slows the car a few minutes later. "Okay, love," she says, "have a great day!"

"I'll try," I say, and slide out, slipping my backpack over my shoulder and giving Mom a wave. Then I hustle inside because having your mom wait while you walk into middle school is getting to be a little embarrassing.

CHAPTER 2

"BROTHER!" YELLS ROBBIE AS HE WALKS into the hallway.

I look up. "Hey there!" I say, smiling at one of my best friends. Our parents call us the Three Musketeers: me, Robbie, and Kai. We've been friends since kindergarten.

Robbie and I start to unpack our bags as we wait for our third musketeer, Kai, to come over.

"Did you finish your math homework?" I ask Robbie. One page was so hard, it made my head hurt.

"Yeah," says Robbie. Robbie is a killer student. He's a jokester, so people are constantly surprised that he reads all the time and is the one all of us go to when we don't know a fact or how something works. Since a lot of people don't think he's too bright, he's also known for really throwing his teachers. In one social studies class Robbie was totally making everyone laugh about the lesson. Last year we were learning about a gubernatorial debate.

"A goober debate?" Robbie asked, knowing full well what he was asking.

"No," Mr. Parks, the social studies teacher, replied. "A gubernatorial debate." He wrote it on the whiteboard.

"You spelled 'goober' wrong!" said Robbie, chuckling.

"Robbie," Mr. Parks warned as kids were laughing. "What is the definition of 'gubernatorial'?"

"It's the debate for the candidates for governor," said Robbie. "And 'gubernatorial' comes from the Latin root word 'gubernare.'"

Kids whistled. "Dude knows his stuff!" said Oscar, two rows up.

Mr. Parks paused for a second, then smirked. "Okay, then, what's the Latin root for 'goober,' Robbie?"

"Oh, that word is actually African in origin," said Robbie, not even blinking. He stared ahead, not joking.

Mr. Parks looked at him, then strode up to the computer. "Let's check that out," he said. He typed the word into the search engine, and sure enough, Robbie was right.

"Dang," said Oscar. "The kid is a genius."

"Robbie," said Mr. Parks, "you amaze me."

"Dudes!" calls Kai now, strolling down the hall.

Kai is really smart too, but in a very different way. Robbie likes to solve things fast, with facts. Kai is known for thinking about things, for really "digging deep," as he likes to say. When the three of us get into it, it's usually me in the middle trying to figure out how to get them to agree.

We don't even get a chance to talk about

anything, even the game last night, before the bell rings for homeroom.

"Ugh," says Kai. "That sound is horrible first thing in the morning."

Robbie and I laugh. "Is it not soothing enough, Kai?" Robbie teases.

Kai gives him a look, and we each go to our homerooms. This year we all have lunch and PE together. "Great," Robbie joked when we first got our schedules, "all three of us are together for our favorite subjects."

I don't have any classes with Kai this year, but after homeroom Robbie and I walk down the hall toward the media studies classroom, the one class the two of us have together.

"Come on in," calls Mrs. Tyler as we all file in toward the desks, which in her room are curved into a horseshoe shape. "Let's get going, class. We have a lot to cover today."

We settle in, glancing up to see the word "Bias" on the whiteboard at the front of the class.

"Okay," says Mrs. Tyler, holding up an armful

of newspapers. "Earlier this week we spoke about our upcoming assignment. We're going to learn about various news sites and how we gather, take in, and then evaluate news. We're going to dive right in. I'm passing these newspapers out now. Everyone, take one off the top of the pile."

"Can't we read these things online?" asks Melanie.

"You can, most of them," says Mrs. Tyler. "But for this exercise we're going to do it the old-fashioned way. With actual paper."

"Ew," says Sam, holding up his white T-shirt sleeve, which is already covered with black print smudges.

"Well, that's a hazard of not reading them online," says Mrs. Tyler. "Okay, let's start with where we were yesterday. Anyone remember the focus of our discussion?"

"Bias," I say.

"That was hard," says Melanie. "Did you look at the whiteboard?"

I scowl at her. Melanie is not a nice person. Or

at least she doesn't act like a nice person. I don't really have a lot of interaction with her, but every time I do, she seems to be obnoxious and acts like she's better than everyone else.

"No," I say. "I pay attention. And I have a good memory."

"No snapping at each other," says Mrs. Tyler. "Melanie, that was uncalled for. Let's bring it back. Yes, bias. Who can give us a good definition of 'bias'? Marcus?"

"You aren't neutral," I say. "You see things or bend things to a certain point of view."

"Excellent," says Mrs. Tyler. "Do you think there's a bias in a newspaper?"

"Yes!" says Robbie.

"Depends on the paper," says Sam.

"Interesting," says Mrs. Tyler. "Go on about that, Sam."

"Well," says Sam. "Some newspapers are kind of known to only present facts one way. Like, they don't really try to present all sides of an issue or a problem."

"Okay," says Mrs. Tyler. "But if it's a news story, how would a bias come in?"

The class looks at her blankly.

"Let's say," she goes on, "the newspaper is covering a fire in a building in town. How could there be evidence of bias?"

"Someone was a bonehead about setting the fire?" says Michael.

"Usually someone is really boneheaded about setting a fire," says Melanie.

"But," says Mrs. Tyler, ignoring Melanie, "if the newspaper just reports facts, what would be included in the article?"

"Where the fire was!" Sam calls out.

Mrs. Tyler nods. "And?"

"If anyone was hurt, or if there was any damage," says Robbie.

"Yep," says Mrs. Tyler.

"And how many responders were there," adds Robbie. "Like, there were four fire engines, and ambulance and police."

"Definitely," says Mrs. Tyler. "What else?"

"How people there reacted?" says Sara, a quiet girl I know because she plays on the girls' basketball team.

"Can you elaborate?" asks Mrs. Tyler.

Sara glances around. "Like, if people were scared or if they were crying or stuff like that. You usually read about that in an article."

"Reactions," says Mrs. Tyler. "Okay, put a pin in that. Now, everyone, take the newspapers I just handed out. Let's look at front-page stories. Any stories about a fire?"

We all peer at the front pages.

"Yeah!" says Sam. "Big one downtown yesterday."

"Here's one," says Melanie. "But this is about a fire at the railroad station."

"I got one," says Henry, a really funny kid I've known since second grade. "An explosion in another country. That's kind of like a fire, right?"

"Okay," says Mrs. Tyler. "Now come at me. Tell me all the facts from these stories, but one at a time." She goes to the whiteboard.

"Happened in the early morning."

"Affected a deserted building."

"Affected all the trains from New York City east to Long Island."

"There were evacuations."

"Facts," says Mrs. Tyler. "Now read those stories fully."

She waits a few minutes, and the classroom is really quiet. I like it when the classroom is quiet. It's kind of like having space for your mind to wander a little.

"Pop open your computers, please," Mrs. Tyler says. "And type in all the facts you have from each story."

I read through mine again. There was a fire at a warehouse a few towns away. No one was hurt, but the building almost collapsed, and everything inside was destroyed. I read a few paragraphs down. The warehouse had stored all sorts of stuff, but some of it had been building materials for construction sites. Nothing too interesting so far. The fire is under investigation to see what started it.

I type all this out. No real red flags or anything.

"Eyes up!" calls Mrs. Tyler. "Now let's have someone go first. Volunteers?"

I raise my hand.

"Okay, Marcus," says Mrs. Tyler. "First read the headline."

"'Catastrophic Fire Decimates Warehouse,'" I say. "That's pretty dramatic."

Then I read the article out loud. "Well, that was interesting," says Oscar sarcastically, and kids laugh.

Mrs. Tyler ignores him. "Okay, now please tell me your facts," she says, and types them onto the whiteboard.

"Uh, Mrs. Tyler," says Robbie. "He can easily cut and paste them, and you can just put them up there instead of retyping that."

Mrs. Tyler sighs. "Thanks, Robbie, but let's try to tap this out fast since I want to get moving on this unit. Keep going, Marcus."

"There's a fire that's under investigation because they don't know how it started," I say. "The warehouse where the fire happened burned to the ground, and everything inside was destroyed. Luckily, nobody was hurt."

"Okay," says Mrs. Tyler. "Robbie, how about you read your article? I believe it covers the same fire."

Robbie reads his article, which is pretty similar to mine. Then he lists his facts. "So there was a fire. It was in a warehouse. Everything was destroyed and the building almost collapsed. The building was a warehouse for construction materials, and nothing was salvageable. As the cause of the fire is suspicious, it is under investigation."

"Wait," I say. "My article said the fire was under investigation. That article says it was suspicious, which seems like someone set it intentionally."

"Good catch," says Mrs. Tyler. "What is the difference here?"

"Well," I say. "One pretty much says there might be foul play."

"That's a pretty substantial claim, don't you think?" asks Mrs. Tyler.

"Well, they didn't say there was foul play," says Robbie. "They just suggested it."

"That's worse," I say. "One article just reported the facts they had. One is suggesting that something bad went on, like someone actually lit the place on fire."

"Wait," says Sara. "That's assuming a lot. A fire could be under investigation because they just don't know what started it. They might investigate to see if it was something that overheated. That's an accident, not someone purposely lighting a building on fire."

"Maybe one reporter knows more," says Robbie. "Maybe they used the word 'suspicious' because they suspect something happened but they don't really know. Or one reporter was lazy and just didn't report the whole thing."

"So," says Mrs. Tyler, "by reading both articles, what are we left to assume or know?"

"Most people," says Melanie, cutting in, "would

read both articles and assume that no one knows how the fire started, and that's why it's under investigation."

"Assuming and knowing are different things," says Robbie.

Mrs. Tyler flashes a grin. "Absolutely," she says.

"But there's a pretty big difference between the fire starting as an accident and someone committing arson," says Robbie.

Melanie shrugs.

"And that," says Mrs. Tyler, "is the point. The difference in reporting may seem minor, with just a few different words or phrases, but how things are reported has major implications. Now, is one article right and one wrong?"

"No," says Sara. "They are reporting what they know."

"So there's no intent really to mislead?" Mrs. Tyler asks.

"Probably not," says Robbie.

"Well," I say, "we'll have to see how this unfolds to see if one might have been holding back information on purpose. Or if one was suggesting something sketchy to get people to keep reading."

Just then the bell rings. "Exactly!" says Mrs. Tyler. "The plot will continue the next time we meet!"

CHAPTER 3

I'M ALREADY STARTING TO LOSE SOME
steam by the time I head to lunch. I was up early
for baseball practice, getting a whole workout done before school. Plus, I have a late lunch
period, so it's practically midafternoon already.

I rip open my lunch bag, dive in, and start inhal-
ing my sandwich.

"Dude, slow down," says Kai. "You are about to
eat a turkey sandwich whole."

"I'm hungry!" I say, swallowing a bunch of let-
tuce.

Kai shakes his head as he opens his salad. Kai always eats healthy stuff. "You are what you eat" is his mantra.

The last time he said that, Robbie said, "Well, I guess I'm a chip. You should call me Chip." "Chip" is the funniest name ever for Robbie, so we all laughed, but now we call him Chip at lunch.

"Hey, Chip," I say as Robbie slides into the seat next to me.

"Hay is for horses," says Robbie. His dad always says that too. We always say hello to Robbie's dad instead of "hey."

"Well, then hello, sir," I say.

"How's the day going, gentlemen?" Robbie asks.

I shrug. "Normal stuff, I guess," I say.

"I have a test in language arts next week," says Kai. "I mean, it's language arts. Arts. What is the point of testing me?"

"So they can see what you've learned?" says Robbie. "How else are they going to do it?"

"They should be teaching me how to read. I should be learning because it's cool, not learning to do well on a test. There is so much skill-and-drill at school," says Kai, shaking his head.

"Kai, I'd like to welcome you to the world," says Robbie, "where we test everything and grade it, and that's how you get into college."

I laugh. Robbie is such a bottom-line guy.

"Skill-and-drill is sometimes useful," I say. "I get out there every day and practice baseball. Those drills are the ones that get me sharp. It's not fun, but you need to do it."

"Well, in baseball I can see that working," says Kai. "You're training your body to act or react in certain ways. But training your mind? There's no right or wrong way to think."

"Uh, you mean there's no one way to solve a math problem?" asks Robbie. "Like, two plus two can sometimes be . . . something other than four?"

"That's a ridiculous example," says Kai. "I mean in terms of how you interpret something you read. We could all watch a movie and see different things in it, or feel different ways about it."

"Yeah," Robbie replies, "but if we were drilled

on it, all three of us would say, 'This is a movie about kids who are really bad baseball players who are put on a rotten team and have to compete and somehow pull it off.' There are facts in there. Beyond that there's room, of course, to talk about how those kids feel, but that's not the goal if you just want to know if you understand the framework."

"Guys," I say, "this is getting deep. Also, we haven't watched *The Bad News Bears* in years."

Kai shrugs. "We should watch it again. You going to basketball today?" he asks.

"Yeah," I say. "We have our first game of the season coming up."

"Cool," Kai says. "Home?"

I nod, knowing Kai and Robbie will come. My crew is good like that. They're always around me.

"Trivia," says Robbie. He loves trivia. Usually it's about sports stats or something. "What do you like better, basketball or baseball?"

"That's not trivia," I say. "That's a question."

I'm annoyed with that question too, especially

coming from Robbie, who knows perfectly well how I feel.

"Robbie," says Kai. "Not cool to bait him."

"Sorry," says Robbie. "I know, and I didn't mean anything by it. I was just wondering if you were more in basketball mode now, since you are in season and baseball has kind of wrapped."

"How about," says Kai, "'Are you excited about basketball starting, Marcus?'"

Robbie sighs. "Okay, okay. Are you excited about basketball?"

I shoot Kai a look. Sometimes Kai and I do that, and it's weird but awesome because he sometimes knows exactly how I'm thinking. Kai is the friend you want because he looks out for his friends, and I never question if he has my back. He always does.

"Yeah, I think we have a good shot this season," I say. "We're all working hard, but we'll see."

Robbie nods. "Cool."

Kai leans over and takes a book from his backpack. "I still can't believe I'm going to get quizzed on this," he says.

"Want help?" I ask, peering at the book. I haven't read it yet.

"I don't even know what the teacher's going to ask," Kai says, frowning. "I read it. I didn't skip any chapters or anything. I guess I'm good?"

We all nod.

"Three more periods to go," says Robbie, glancing at the clock.

I take out my phone. We're only allowed to use our phones at lunch. If you're caught with a phone in class, the roof will really come down on you. The weird thing is that, since kids are only allowed to officially use them at lunch, you just see table after table of quiet kids, staring at their phones instead of talking. But the Three Musketeers are always talking.

I glance at a message from my dad. Have fun at basketball. I'll be there to pick you up tonight. Miss you. PS Don't forget to pass!

My dad is really tough on me about baseball. He rules me hard in the mornings during our practice sessions. But he's still my dad, and I know he feels like I do, that it's sometimes really sad that we aren't all under the same roof at night. Normally he wouldn't send me texts like this just to check in, but I've been talking about my feelings a little more now that I'm meeting with Gary, and Gary told me that sometimes I have to tell people what I need from them instead of leaving them guessing.

It's almost like Robbie is reading my mind at this moment, because he says, "You know, Marcus, I think you're great at everything you try, including basketball. You're gonna kill it out there on the court."

Kai smiles like a proud parent.

"I love you too, Robbie," I say in a high, teasing voice, and grab his last chip.

CHAPTER 4

I'M ALWAYS GLAD TO HEAR THE LAST BELL
of the day. It's a relief, like, *Okay, you're done,*
and we all scatter for buses and cars and practices. Or sofas.

I head to the locker room to get ready for basketball practice. Of course the first person I see
sitting on the bench is James. It isn't like he's
my nemesis or anything, but James and I really
don't like each other. Unfortunately, we see each
other a lot because we also play competitive baseball together. We respect each other because we're

both solid players, but he can be a real jerk. I try to take the high road, but sometimes he makes it hard.

Today he just nods at me, and I nod back, throwing my stuff into a locker. Then I change into my shorts and take my basketball sneakers from my bag. People think it's crazy that basketball players don't want to get their sneaks dirty, but that isn't really why we don't like wearing them outside. When you play on a basketball court, your grip is important, so nobody wants to wear out the tread on their shoes. You want a good grip.

"C'mon, boys," calls Coach Fuller. "We have work to do today."

We all hurry to finish getting dressed, and slam the lockers shut as we head into the gym.

"Okay," Coach says. "Let's get to it with drills. Then I can split up the squads."

My friend Jayden waves to me.

"Hey!" I call as I jog up next to him.

We play well together and are hoping to be on the same squad. Coach Fuller groups the practice squads as we play together on the court. I'm a pretty good rebounder and, if I do say so myself, a great defender, but my shots aren't always as solid as they could be. And then there is the bigger issue. Literally.

I'm not a tall kid. I'm average height, according to every height chart and my doctor. I'm going to be straight-out honest and say that being shorter than other kids makes it hard in sports. Especially if basketball is one of your sports. There have been plenty of famous shorter pro basketball players. There have even been epic shorter players, like Keith Jennings, Monte Towe, and Charlie Criss. They're all under 5'10", which is not that tall, especially for a basketball player. But being shorter means you have to work harder. To go up against another player who is a foot taller than you, you need to have rocket springs in your feet to get into the air, and you really have to have great ball-handling skills to be able to get around them.

I know what people see when I step onto a basketball court. It's, *Oh, that shortie isn't going*

- -

to be able to play. Or, *Don't worry about blocking that one.* I like that I can surprise them. There is also a lot of, *Wait, that's the kid who plays baseball. What's he doing here?* I don't like that. What I like is when it gets to, *Well, what do you know, that short baseball kid can press the court with the best of them.*

The first game of the season is always a big one. It sets the tone for the team, kind of announces who stands out, how we play together. Word gets around fast, like, *Hey, did you see how the Warriors played? They were ridiculously bad. They aren't going to have a great season at all.*

Now, that isn't exactly fair. I mean, we have eighteen games this season, and there will probably be a game or two that we just won't play well. My dad always says that about baseball, too, that you can't judge an entire team on just one game. But people do still judge.

My mind is really wandering during drills. With baseball I trained myself to just cut my thoughts off, to concentrate on the game. I can block out the noise. Usually. But I'm still learning how to do that with basketball, and other stuff too.

Gary helps a lot with this. I admit that at first I was on the fence about going to see a therapist. It seemed weird to talk to this new guy about what was really going on in my mind. But he helps me. It's cool to be able to just say what I'm thinking and feeling without having to worry that someone like Dad will say, *Well, don't worry; that's not going to happen.* Or Mom will say, *And even if that happens, we love you.* Or even Robbie asking, *But why do you care?* With Gary nothing is off-limits, and I'm not judged. I can say, *I think this kid is awful*, and he won't say, *Well, maybe you have to get to know him* or anything like that. He'll just listen to why I think that kid deserves to be looked at sideways.

Coach glances at his tablet. "Let's start it off like this, gentlemen. I'm going to split you into squads." I look down until I hear "Stroman" and then follow where he's pointing. I give a little sigh of relief, because it seems like I'm on the A squad with Jayden.

I get a little boost from that, and I play hard.

"That's it, Marcus," Coach calls. "Don't wait for that ball to come down. I want to see your feet in the air as it goes in, so you're ready to grab it for the rebound."

"He needs to work on getting it in," mutters James.

"James, I'm the coach," Coach Fuller says, "so let's keep opinions to ourselves and play our own game, okay? And if you want to offer opinions, my opinion is that he should be rebounding a ball you get in, not a shot you're missing."

I try not to smirk. James has a way of always setting himself up.

Jayden laughs out loud and slaps me on the back.

"All right," says Coach Fuller. "Let's go. We're going to work on ballhandling today. Three on two, two on one, and one on one." He blows his whistle.

This drill means you're split into offense and defense. In three on two, there are three offense and two defense, and the person in the middle passes to the wing. Then you switch positions, so defense turns into offense. It sounds confusing, but it makes a lot of sense when you do it. Essentially you flip playing offense and defense so you sharpen your skills on each.

I start on offense as I run down the court. Basketball is a fast game, up and down the court, changing from offense to defense with the pass of a ball, which is one of the reasons I love it. The pace is awesome.

We're sweating pretty good when we finally finish practice. I gulp down half my water bottle and look up to see my dad waiting by the gym door. I give a little wave, then grab my bag from the locker room. I take off my shoes, put on some slides, and carry my sneakers as I walk over to him. As expected, he rolls his eyes.

"In my day you got your shoes dirty," he says.

"In my day you worry about tread, not dirt," I say, shrugging.

"Don't step in any puddles with those," says Dad, pointing to my socked feet in the slides. He waves to Coach Fuller as we head to the car.

"How was practice?" Dad asks as he pulls out of the parking lot.

"Pretty good," I say.

Dad nods. "You look like you got in a good workout."

I wipe my forehead, which is still sweaty. "Without doubt," I say.

Dad is humming as he drives me to Mom's house. If this were baseball practice, Dad would ask a bunch of questions. It's not that he isn't interested in basketball. He likes the game a lot, and he's happy I'm on the team. But I think Dad is glad that I'm playing and keeping active and fit through the winter because that's good for baseball. This bothers me. It bothers me a lot.

"Dad," I say. "Kai is a really good musician, right?"

Dad looks puzzled. "Yeah, he is. The kid has a lot of talent."

"So do you think he's going to be a professional musician?" I ask.

Dad shrugs. "Maybe. But he's really good at puzzling things out, fixing things. He might be a mechanic, or an engineer. Who knows?"

Exactly. That's the thing: a lot of people I know are good at a lot of things. But for me it's always, *He's a great baseball player. He's going to be a professional baseball player.* Nobody's walking around saying Kai can only be a musician.

I think about that as I look out the window. Dad pulls into Mom's driveway. At this time of year it's already getting dark in late afternoon, and the lamps inside reflect off the windows of the house. Dad sighs. "Tell your sister this house is lit up like a Christmas tree. She needs to turn off some of those lights!"

"Will do," I say. "Talk to you later, Dad. Love you."

Dad reaches over and gives me a hug. "Love you too. See you in the morning, son."

Dad waits in the car until I'm inside the house. It's a little weird to get dropped off by a parent at your own house. It isn't that Dad never comes inside or anything, but tonight he's headed straight to work. It's just strange to have your parents carpool between houses. If we all lived together, Dad would zip in to grab a bottle of water or something. I lean against the door, sad for a second, until Sabria opens her bedroom door and yells, "Is that you, Marcus?"

"Yeah!" I call up.

"Mom says do your homework and set the table. She'll be home soon," yells Sabria. Then she slams her door shut.

I roll my eyes. Sabria is always trying to order me around. I walk into the kitchen and realize I can grab a snack without being ratted out, so I snag a bag of chips. "Here's to you, Robbie," I say, digging in.

"You aren't supposed to be eating that," Sabria says. I spin around. I didn't hear her come downstairs.

"Are you spying on me?" I ask.

"No," she says. "Mom always asks if I check on you when I'm here watching you. So I'm checking on you."

"You aren't 'watching' me," I say. "You aren't the babysitter."

"Yeah, I am," says Sabria. Then she reaches over and grabs a handful of chips for herself. "It's weird to have Dad drop you off, right?"

I look up, surprised. "Definitely," I say. "Aren't we supposed to be used to it by now?"

Sabria shrugs. "I don't know."

We sit there eating chips for a while, and the only sound is the bag rustling and us chomping. The thing is, as annoying as my sister is, she's the one who's there, going through the same things I am. She understands a lot of stuff about me that nobody else can.

"What's bugging you?" she asks.

"Nothing," I say.

She looks at me like, *Really?*

I sigh. "It's just that I really like basketball."

"And that's a problem?" she asks.

"No," I say. "But nobody wants to talk to me about basketball. They all just think it's a hobby or something."

Sabria nods. "So you think you could be a pro basketball player, like everyone thinks you can be a pro baseball player?"

"Maybe," I say.

"Well, then tell them it means a lot to you," says Sabria. "Or let them see you train as hard as you train for baseball. Show them."

I nod slowly. Maybe she's right. Maybe I just need to show everyone how much it means to me. I breathe out slowly. The worst thing about an older sister is that a lot of the time, she's 100 percent right.

CHAPTER 5

THE NEXT MORNING, AS USUAL, I HAVE
training with Dad. He had an overnight shift,
so he comes to Mom's house straight from work,
right at our usual time. Mom is always up early
too, and she made some extra coffee for him.

"You made Dad coffee?" I ask.

"Yep," she says. "And good morning to you."

"Good morning," I say, tying my shoes, getting
ready to head outside.

I guess she sees me thinking about this,
because she shrugs and says, "My coffee is bet-

ter than the cup he gets from the deli."

It isn't that I want my parents to hate each other. I have friends with parents like that, and it's a nightmare. Those parents won't even be in the same room together. But in a way I wonder if that's a little clearer. When my parents do nice things for each other, sometimes I think, *Well, can't you just do that more and stay married?* We've had that conversation before. Mom always says that she and Dad are nicer to each other as parents who aren't married.

I sigh and wave. "Here I go," I say, and open the back door. A lot of people think it's nuts that I train every morning, but I've been training every morning for as long as I can remember. My dad has me throw, run, and do core training. Like, sometimes when it snows, he has me load a sled with weight and run up and down the street pulling it. It's just something I do to get myself into peak physical shape. My friends are half-impressed and half-shocked that I have to get dressed and out of bed early every morning, even on weekends.

"Good morning, son," says Dad, pulling a bucket of balls from the shed in the backyard.

"Morning, Dad," I say, putting on my glove.

"Let's start with some throws," says Dad. He squats down and waits for me to toss some pitches, which I do, one after another. Dad usually times our practice sessions, and I wait for him to set the pace. Depending on how I throw, he'll either quickly or slowly move on to something else, like running or weights.

My throws are pretty solid this morning. It feels good to see that I'm still in my zone, even in the off-season. Indoor training will start soon for the baseball team, but right now I can feel less pressure since there aren't any games. But Dad is watching, and with Dad watching, you do your best.

Actually, that isn't really fair. Sure, Dad expects my best with everything, but I also expect myself to do my best. If it were up to me, I might skip a few practices—there's no way Dad would agree to that—but it's not like I get out on the field and think, *Eh, whatever.* I push myself too. Gary tells me that's okay, but I also have to learn to accept. I can tell myself I should pitch no-hitters every game, but that's not realistic. I can try, but I need to understand that even if I don't meet that bar, I'm still giving it my best. That sounds like very fair and practical advice, but sometimes it's hard to remember in real life. I'm working on it.

"Ready to change it up?" Dad asks, standing up slowly.

I breathe out. "Okay," I say, following him to the shed. He comes out with some cones and sets them up in a zigzag line.

I know this drill. I run around the cones, turning my body quickly to hit the tight spots. Then, at the end of the line, I drop and do push-ups, then flip and do sit-ups. When I spring up after the first set, Dad nods and says, "Twenty-four more."

As I go through the drills, I wonder about the dads who plunk down next to their kids and play video games or just read the news or whatever else my friends' parents do in the morning. Robbie's dad makes awesome pancakes. He jokes that by the time Robbie comes downstairs, they're always cold, but Robbie eats them anyway.

Kids say to me, "Wait, your dad makes you work out *every* morning?"

It isn't that he *makes* me do it. If I say, "I am not doing this ever again," there will certainly be a discussion, but I have a choice in the matter. My dad set up a program to support me in getting to be the best in my game.

It's complicated, for sure.

After I finish my last set of sit-ups, I roll over and fall face-first into the grass.

"And with that I wish you a great day at school, son," says my dad, laughing.

"Ugh," I moan, and get up slowly.

"Any tests today?" Dad asks.

"Nope, normal day," I say.

Dad gives me a hug. "Never settle for normal. Make it extraordinary!"

"Okay," I say, not really convincingly. I wave and start to head inside to shower and get breakfast. Then I stop. I jog over to the shed and grab a basketball. Then I run to the front of the house.

Maybe I have to show everyone that basketball means something to me.

Bounce, bounce. I dribble the ball in the driveway. Dad is headed toward his car, and he looks up.

"Do you need me?" he asks.

"Always," I say, joking. Then I start bouncing the ball again, getting ready to shoot into the net that's above the garage door.

"You getting in a few shots?" Dad asks, puzzled.

"Yep," I say. "I practice baseball every morning. Why aren't I practicing basketball, too?"

Dad looks like he's going to say something, then stops. "Fair," he says, watching me. With baseball Dad would yell, "Line it up!" or "Concentrate," but for a few minutes he just watches me dribble from side to side, then shoot.

"Nice shot!" he says, smiling. Then he waves. "Don't make yourself late for school!"

I nod and go for the rim again, slam in a shot and hang on a little bit.

"And don't show off!" I hear him yell right before he shuts the car door.

I decide I need to hit twelve shots in a row before I can go inside.

Twelve shots don't sound like a lot. Until you try to hit a dozen shots in enough time to get yourself ready for school and not be late.

I get to eight hoops without too much of a problem, and then I just can't get another in. I'm getting frustrated, so I do my breathing exercise. I breathe in through my nose counting to three, then out through my mouth counting to three. Then I breathe in for four and out for four. I'm breathing out for six before I feel calm again. Then I shoot, and sink it in.

Twelve into the bucket. *Maybe tomorrow I should do twenty,* I think.

I put the ball away, then sprint into the house.

"So now we're practicing two sports in the morning?" asks Mom, who's making eggs. She sees me look at the pan. "No time for pancakes this morning, especially if you're squeezing in more practice time."

I shrug. "It's basketball season. Got to put in the effort."

"Effort is good," she agrees. "And getting to school on time is good too. Hop it up there, kiddo. You definitely need a shower."

I chug some water and rush around. I only added a few minutes to my morning practice, but it feels good. If basketball is important to me, then I need to make it a priority.

This plan to practice two sports in the morning feels really good until I slide into my seat for my first class of the day, media studies. I'm tired already.

"Did you stay up late?" asks Robbie, who sits next to me.

"I did a double workout this morning," I say.

Robbie raises his eyebrows. "You make me feel like such a slacker."

"Oh really? How late were you up doing homework?" I ask.

"Midnight," says Robbie. "I have a math test."

I smile. "You are no slacker, my friend."

Mrs. Tyler is setting up something on the whiteboard and doesn't seem to notice that we're all seated even before the bell rings.

"Oh!" she says, looking up. "Good morning, class. I'm a little distracted here, getting ready to go right into our big project for the semester."

We all wait.

"We've been talking about news, facts, how things are reported, and how they are perceived. I keep saying that we have a big project coming up, and we're there. For this project we're going to flip it a little bit to get behind the scenes. We are going to report the news now."

We all wait some more. No one seems especially excited about reporting the news.

"We're going to publish our own newspaper," Mrs. Tyler says proudly.

We all look at each other.

"Us?" asks Oscar. "As in we're going to do it?"

"Yes," says Mrs. Tyler. "That's exactly what I mean. We are, as of today, in the newspaper business. You will all be discussing what should be covered, reporting the stories, editing the stories, taking pictures that go with the stories, laying out the pages, and publishing a newspaper."

"What is the newspaper called?" asks Melanie.

"Up to you," says Mrs. Tyler. "This is your project for the semester. After we produce a full newspaper, another class will take over and will probably make some changes. It will be interesting for us to step back and see what direction another class might take. Then it will be our turn again. So we'll tag-team through the semester."

"So we go first?" asks Robbie.

"First out of the gate," says Mrs. Tyler. "Where do you think we should start?"

The class is quiet. Then Sara raises her hand.

"I work on the school newspaper," she says. "First of all, is this a competing paper?"

"Good question," says Mrs. Tyler. "When you

go to a store or go online, do you see a few different newspapers?"

Everyone nods.

"This is not a situation where there's just one newspaper," Mrs. Tyler says. "And there shouldn't be. The school newspaper does a fine job serving our school community. They already started publishing this year on a weekly basis, and we aren't going to take that over. Our intent isn't to 'take them on,' either. We can exist side by side. And I'm hoping we see that there should be alternate sources of news so that we thoroughly cover everything."

"But shouldn't we at least look at what they're doing so we can take a different direction?" asks Robbie.

"That's a good idea," says Mrs. Tyler. She walks over to her desk and picks up a copy of the school paper, the *Warrior Writes*, and holds it up.

"First of all, that is a terrible name," says Sam. "We need something much better and much cooler if we're going to get kids to read it."

Mrs. Tyler grins. "Okay," she says, typing out "New Name" on the board.

"And we should decide what we cover," says Sara. "The *Warrior* covers everything, from news to opinions to reviews of restaurants and movies."

"Also a good point," says Mrs. Tyler. "And let's keep Sara's voice in mind here, since she works on the *Warrior* and does a great job."

Sara nods. "It might be weird to work on both," she says. "And I'm a little concerned about the way kids are talking right now, saying that no one seems to read it."

"We do read it," says Robbie. "When there are stacks of it in the cafeteria, kids grab it and flip through it."

"But we don't rely on it," says Melanie.

Everyone turns to look at her.

"Well," she says, "a good newspaper is one you look to for news and information. We read the *Warrior* because we're kind of curious who they interview for the Person of the Week column, but no one is reading any breaking news in there."

"*Is* there breaking news at our school?" asks Oscar, and we all laugh.

"These are all good points," says Mrs. Tyler. "Let's dive in here. I'd like to get the first issue of the paper printed within a few weeks. The first thing to decide is what kind of paper we'd like to publish. All news? Some news, some reviews? Let's break out what sections we think this thing should have."

"Definitely news," says Melanie, and everyone nods.

"Opinion pieces?" asks Sara.

"Why?" asks Mrs. Tyler. "I think it's a good idea, but why do you?"

"Because there aren't a ton of platforms for students to have their voices heard."

"Excellent point."

"Well, that seems silly," says Melanie. "I mean, you can't honestly say there aren't a million platforms on social media. And everyone has an opinion on social media. You don't even need to write an opinion. You just do a like or a thumbs-up, and that's your opinion right there, recorded for everyone to see what you support."

"Or not," says Robbie, and I stifle a laugh. Robbie claimed it was a mistake, but over the summer he liked a post from this girl Jennifer. We thought Robbie had a crush on Jennifer because he then liked almost every post from her. All those little thumbs popped up when he liked them, and we thought that was hilarious.

Unfortunately, Robbie didn't thoroughly read one post from Jennifer before he liked it, and it was about how much she was in love . . . with a guy named Luis. So then Robbie unliked the post, which was worse because then everyone only talked about how Robbie had unliked Jennifer because she liked another guy. It was a whole mess that Kai and I ribbed Robbie for, but he was really embarrassed. Good thing it happened over the summer, because a lot gets forgotten over the summer.

I decide to jump in before anyone remembers and brings it up. "We should definitely have a sports section," I say. "A lot of people read news-papers just for the sports coverage."

"Okay," says Mrs. Tyler, writing that down. "How about an entertainment section too?"

"People do care about movie reviews and show reviews," says Michael.

"Why do you think they care?" asks Mrs. Tyler.

"Let's say you're on the fence about down-loading a song, or going to see a movie," says Michael. "Sometimes a review can help you make that decision."

"Bingo," says Mrs. Tyler. "And that means those reviews can be pretty influential, right?"

"Yeah," says Michael. "But they should be fair. So if someone in here writes them, they should be able to be fair about it."

"Fairness matters in news," says Mrs. Tyler. "Let's keep that front of mind."

By the end of the period we have a list of sec-tions for the paper.

"Okay," says Mrs. Tyler as the bell rings, "homework is to read the latest edition of the *Warrior*, which is out today, and come prepared to discuss it."

An easy homework assignment. This is turning into a good day.

CHAPTER 6

WINTER PRACTICE HASN'T STARTED YET
for baseball, so I only have basketball practice a
few times a week, and one game a week. It's kind
of nice not to have something every single day,
especially because the teachers seem to pile on a
ton of homework this time of year.

After school Mom drives me to Gary's office,
which is good because I haven't seen him in a few
weeks. He was on vacation. When I walk in, he
high-fives me.

"I've missed you!" he says, smiling.

I grin. "Don't worry. I've saved many problems for you."

I wave to Mom in the waiting room and follow him into his office. Mom and Dad sometimes come in with me for my sessions with Gary, but most of the time it's just me.

Gary chuckles and we settle in. Usually I sit on the comfy green chair in his office, and he sits in a leather one across from me, but sometimes I wander around as I talk. His office is filled with pictures of athletes because he's a mental-health coach specializing in sports stress, which is when you have anxiety about how you're performing on a field or court. It's all tied up with anxiety you might be having off the field or court too, and Gary's job is to help people unravel that anxiety and try to manage it.

Gary's job isn't to erase the anxiety. You can't really stop it entirely. I probably won't step onto a mound without feeling a little twinge in my stomach or a little flutter. But I'm learning how to breathe it out, block out some of it, and deal with it so it doesn't get in the way of how I play, or how I feel about playing.

Gary waits for me to start talking, as usual. I'm used to adults asking me questions and me replying respectfully, so it's still a little weird that he just sits there and lets me jump in wherever I want. Sometimes I just sit there for a few minutes, gathering my thoughts. And sometimes I don't really want to talk at all. It's all cool with Gary.

"How was your vacation?" I ask.

"Great!" says Gary. "It's really essential to pull the plug, you know? Just take off, take a break, leave a lot of stuff you usually worry about behind. It recharges you."

I think about that for a second. "But we only take vacations a few times a year."

"True," says Gary. "Most people only take a few vacations, if they can. Those are our major recharging options. But we have weekends. And we have moments sometimes, right? When I take an hour to go for a run, I can shut off my phone and my email and not talk to anyone. I just run and listen to my own thoughts. It's not the same as a vacation, but you can try to get some little breaks in. And you should."

"When I'm playing, I concentrate," I say. "When I do homework, I concentrate. When I hang out with my friends . . . I guess it's a little break?"

"It is," says Gary. "And those are needed. But sometimes you need to formalize that break a little bit. You need to completely cut off your normal routine and change things up."

I nod. Gary waits. I have a lot to say, but sometimes I just like sitting here with him in the quiet.

"So," I say. "How do I tell people something is important to me? Like, not just say, 'Oh, hey, this is important to me' but really reinforce that?"

Gary sits back. "Well, you're going in the right direction. First you tell them. And, hopefully, they listen."

"Listening and believing are two different things," I say.

"Excellent point," he says. "Sometimes people

hear what they want to hear. Is that happening to you?"

I nod.

He waits.

"Everyone sees me as a baseball player," I say. "And that's cool. But I'm more than that."

"You absolutely are," says Gary.

"But it's like you get tagged as something, right?" I say. "I'm the baseball player who might be able to go pro. I'm supposed to be obsessed with baseball."

"You are pretty invested in baseball," says Gary.

"Well, yeah," I say. "It's big for me. I don't deny that. But there's so much more than baseball. I can write pretty well. I like playing around with music. And I'm a good basketball player. I'm a pretty good tennis player, too."

"That's great," says Gary. "We should celebrate everything we can do."

"Okay," I say, then stop. "That sounds like something my grandmother would say in a cheesy card that she sends me."

"Yeah," says Gary, laughing. "But it's true!"

I roll my eyes. "So why do people see me as just a baseball player? It's so frustrating."

"Can you give me an example?" asks Gary. "Or is this a general thing?"

"Both," I say. "First example. Every morning, I practice baseball with my dad. It's intense. But when I started to practice basketball in the mornings too, everyone was surprised. Why would they be surprised?"

"People are sometimes surprised by new routines."

"You just said that changing up routines is good," I say. "But in this case, when I changed it up for basketball, everyone was surprised that I care about things besides baseball. But I do!"

"That's really healthy, Marcus," Gary says. "There's a whole world out there."

"And that world might not even include baseball," I say. "What if after all this, I don't make the pros? Or I make the pros and am terrible? Or I hate it? What then?"

"All good questions," says Gary.

"Shouldn't I have other things that make me happy besides baseball?"

"What do you think?" asks Gary.

"Yes," I say. "I think I should."

"So," says Gary, "the issue is that you're pretty confident about not just zeroing in on baseball all the time, but people aren't listening?"

"Yes!" I say, a little loudly.

"Why do you think they aren't listening?"

I've been thinking about this a lot. "Because it's easier to just see me as one thing."

"Go on," says Gary.

"I'm the baseball player. Boom. Tag. Everything is about baseball, and everything else is just a little hobby or not important. Because if one of those other things starts to get in the way of baseball, or take over for baseball, well, then we have a different course."

"BAM," says Gary.

I jump a little.

"People get labeled," says Gary. "Sometimes

they get put into little buckets, and that's their image or how we're supposed to think of them. It's easier. But people are complicated and multi-dimensional."

"Well," I say. "Just to take that on, sometimes there are people who are all about one thing. There are some athletes or musicians or even business-people who are all in." I think of some athletes who say they never take a break, never eat junk food, and who brag about missing things like holidays, giving up everything and living only for their sport.

"A lot of things take sacrifice," says Gary. "Not just in sports or music but in regular life, too. But it's about balancing those priorities and sacrifices, so that it works for you in a way that also keeps your priorities in check."

I think about that.

"Can I have more than one priority?"

"Of course!" says Gary. "I mean, one priority would be a pretty boring life, right? If your one priority was getting the most ice cream you could in every situation, what do you think would happen?"

"I would totally get sick of ice cream," I say.

"Exactly," says Gary.

"I would also probably throw up." Gary laughs. I think for a minute. "So am I going to get sick of baseball?"

"What do you think?" Gary asks.

"No!" I practically yell. "I love baseball. It's great. And I'm great at it. I want to play. And I want to play well."

"Okay," says Gary, flat-toned. He reacts like I said I like chocolate pudding more than vanilla pudding, not like I said "This means so much to me." I'm used to that with Gary. Sometimes he doesn't have a reaction because he doesn't want to influence how I'm feeling or what I'm about to say.

I lean forward in my chair.

"Sometimes I want things other than baseball," I say, trying to clarify what's running through my head. "Sometimes I like being the basketball player. Or the future music engineer. But people just refuse to see those as possibilities."

"Do they refuse to see it, or are you not showing them as possibilities?" asks Gary. "Genuine question. Have you said, for instance, 'This is important to me' to your family?"

"They should know," I say, and the minute I say it, I know Gary will call me on it.

"We've talked about this, Marcus," Gary says. "Your parents and other family members know you well, but they don't always know exactly what's going on inside your head. You have to talk about it to help them understand."

"And if they still don't understand?" I ask, thinking that if I tell Dad I love basketball a lot, he'll just say, *Okay, that's good.*

"If they don't, then that's for them to deal with. But you put it out there. And what you believe, you believe. No one can change that."

I think about that. "I believe what I believe," I repeat.

"If your dad thinks basketball isn't a big deal

but you believe it's important, then it's important to you. And that's what matters," Gary says.

I nod.

"We have a lot of things I ask you to think about and repeat," says Gary. "This week I'd like you to keep saying 'What I believe is important.'"

"What I believe is important," I say. Then I let some air out through my mouth.

Now I just have to figure out what I believe.

CHAPTER 7

AT DINNER, MOM, SABRIA, AND I TALK ABOUT
a long weekend we have coming up next month.

"I was thinking about this," says Mom, looking really excited. "What if we take the camping trip we didn't get to take this summer?"

"The one we couldn't take because of Marcus's baseball-palooza?" asks Sabria, giving me a glare.

"It would have been too hot anyway," I say. "And you hate bugs. There are more bugs in summer."

Mom decides to ignore our bickering.

"There's an amazing park about two hours

away. The fall foliage is supposed to be at its peak around the time you have off from school, so it would be a great time to go."

"And what exactly would we do besides look at the leaves?" I ask, thinking of a very long drive to nowhere.

"We'd connect with nature," Mom says. "Listen to the sounds, breathe in really crisp, clean air."

I look at her like, *Are you serious?*

"Didn't the tent rip the last time we tried to go camping?" asks Sabria.

We sleep in a tent in the backyard a lot, at Mom's house and at Dad's. It's pretty fun, but the upside of sleeping in a tent in your backyard is that you can run into the house and get a snack. And the last time we tried to leave the backyard and go on a real camping trip, our tent *did* rip, on the beach, during a rainy day when Mom thought the storm might clear out. We ended up driving home pretty fast.

"I think it's time we try again with an overnight trip," says Mom.

Sabria and I look at each other, recognizing the

tone of Mom's voice. When you hear that tone, you step back, because there is no changing her mind.

I sigh.

"Well," says Sabria, "at least we'll have s'mores."

Mrs. Tyler is trying to get us to stop talking in class, and she's getting frustrated, so she just turns off the lights. We all look up.

"Well, that got your attention," she says. "Now let's proceed without loud voices here."

We settle down.

Things were a little heated because we're assigning stories for the newspaper we're producing for media studies. The newspaper is going to be called the *Warrior Times*. It isn't the most clever name, in my opinion, especially because it seems like it's about news from the warrior times of ancient Greece, but that's a whole other fight.

"The issue," says Mrs. Tyler, "is what qualifies a reporter to cover a subject. The reporter for a news story should be impartial, which means they can cover something fairly, without interjecting their own views. For example, would we have Marcus cover the baseball game he played in?"

"No!" everyone yells.

"Hey!" I say. "I can be impartial about how we played. Players aren't completely blind to how we do in a game. When we don't play well, we know, trust me."

"Fair point," says Mrs. Tyler. "Still, do you think it's fair to cover yourself?"

"I think I could give a fair assessment of my performance," I say confidently.

"He could," says Robbie, backing me up. "But Marcus isn't a good example of what most people can do."

I whip my head around. "What?"

"You were trained to take your playing seriously and evaluate yourself. You can step away from what you did," says Robbie. "Most people aren't like that. If you asked my dad how the pancakes he made on the weekend tasted, he'd tell you they were the bomb."

"Wait, they aren't?" I ask.

"They are the worst," says Robbie. "Why do you think I don't rush down to eat them? But if you told my dad they were terrible, you'd hurt his feelings. He truly thinks he could be Chef of the Year."

"But why wouldn't you just tell him the truth?" asks Melanie.

"He's my dad," says Robbie. "I don't know about your family, but in my family we don't try to insult or hurt each other."

Melanie rolls her eyes.

"When it comes to my family," Robbie adds, "I'm not neutral. Marcus is like a freak of a baseball player. He's not a normal person you can compare things to."

"Thanks," I say.

"You know what I mean," says Robbie, looking at me.

"Okay," says Mrs. Tyler, jumping in. "So let's think this through. To cover a subject, you should know something about it, right? You wouldn't want me covering a basketball game because I don't really understand basketball or how you keep score. I don't even know how many points you get for a basket."

The class laughs. "Two!" yells Sam. "Unless you're behind the three-point line. Then it's three."

"Thank you for explaining that to me," says Mrs. Tyler. "But you still wouldn't want me covering a game. So you have to have some experience or understand what you're covering but still be able to be impartial. Do we all agree on that?"

Everyone nods.

"Progress!" says Mrs. Tyler. "Let's use that as we assign stories, okay?" She goes to the whiteboard, where the proposed stories for the first issue are all listed.

We're covering the usual stuff, like a new teacher, a new outdoor learning classroom planned for the spring, new mandatory study halls, and the fall performances of the drama club, choir, orchestra, and band. For sports stories we'll cover the upcoming volleyball tournament, basketball games for boys and girls, and meets for the swim teams and track teams.

"For a really boring school, there's more stuff going on than I thought," says Sam.

"How are we going to fit this all into a paper?" asks Robbie.

"Good question," says Mrs. Tyler. "Usually a publication has a staff position called the managing editor. That person helps organize things, gets a system in place, and helps coordinate production. I think it would be a good idea if we had a managing editor for this paper to help with things like that. Any volunteers?"

"I'll do it!" says Robbie, and then he stands up.

"Where are you going?" asks Mrs. Tyler as Robbie heads up to the whiteboard.

"I already have some ideas," says Robbie, holding his laptop. Good old Robbie. He has already divided the newspaper into sections and figured out how many words each section can have.

"You just did that?" asks Mrs. Tyler incredulously.

"Yeah," says Robbie. "And we can use this program I found online."

"When did you find this program?" asks Mrs. Tyler.

Robbie looks up sheepishly. "Well, I assumed someone had to when we were discussing this, which is why I was not browsing online but specifically searching for this tool just now."

Mrs. Tyler looks at him for a minute, then shrugs. "Okay, show us what you found."

Robbie shows how we can lay the paper out with a template that lets us put in headlines and photos and can look really professional.

"That seems like it could work really well," says Mrs. Tyler. "Now we just have to get a budget for printing them out."

"Why?" asks Robbie. "We all read things online now. Maybe that's a difference between us and the *Warrior Writes*."

"How do you all feel about that?" asks Mrs. Tyler, turning to the rest of the class.

"It would save paper," says Sara, "which is always a good thing."

"But," says Melanie, "it could delay things. If

you have a phone at lunch, you can read it when we publish, but otherwise you'd need to wait until you get home to look on a computer."

"We have computers in school," says Michael, pointing to the one in front of him.

"But teachers don't let you just read what you want," says Melanie, looking pointedly at Robbie.

"You can read it in study hall," says Robbie, "or in lunch. I don't see technology getting in the way here."

Robbie and Melanie go back and forth a few times before Mrs. Tyler jumps in again and says, "Let's get these stories assigned so we can all start our work."

At this point everyone is vying for a story. My head is still stuck on what my best friend Robbie said a few minutes earlier. "Marcus is like a freak of a baseball player." A freak? Not normal? Does Robbie really see me that way? Does everyone else?

I guess I'm in more of a thought fog than I realized, because the next thing I know, Mrs. Tyler is saying, "Does that work for you, Marcus?" and everyone is looking at me.

"Sure," I say, which is how I end up with the assignment to cover the new outdoor classroom. Thrilling.

I sigh. Gary is right. I need to tell people what I want . . . and don't want.

CHAPTER 8

A FEW MORNINGS LATER I WAKE UP AT Dad's house, so I don't worry about making my bed before I go downstairs for practice. I throw on a hat before I go outside, because the mornings are definitely getting colder, which I hate. I love being outside in the heat. The hotter the better, even though everyone else complains. I do not love the cold at all.

Dad is sitting on the back deck with an enormous coffee cup.

"Ready?" he asks.

I nod and put on my glove. Dad goes down the steps and walks onto the lawn as he always does. Dad's house isn't that big, but it has a big backyard, great for playing sports. The house was built into a little bit of a hill, so the deck is high up, jutting off the house, almost like a platform, with a cool view of the woods behind the house. Also, since it's up high, you can stand under the deck and use a squirt gun, aiming between the wood slats, and get everyone's butts wet when they're sitting out there, but don't ask me how I know that.

I throw to Dad, trying to concentrate. When I practice with Dad in the morning, it's usually quiet, except, of course, when he's yelling about my form. Usually, though, he gives me the drills and I do them. Today we're working on curveballs.

"Your spin," Dad calls.

"Yeah?" I ask.

"Your spin is off," he answers, with a look that says, *Don't you realize that?*

For a pitch, the spin of the ball matters. A lot. In basic terms, the amount a ball spins when it leaves your hand determines where that ball lands, which is essential for a pitcher. Pitchers throw a specific kind of pitch depending on the batter and the outcome they're hoping for. Your spin is determined by where your fingers are placed and how you're holding the ball in the last second or two before it leaves your hand. You use different spins for different pitches. It sounds complicated because it is. You see a pitcher standing on a mound and you might think they're just throwing a ball, but there's a lot going on.

Dad gets up and puts the ball into my hand. "Show me your grip," he says.

I choke the ball, which you're supposed to do for a curveball, then turn my wrist, showing him how I'm snapping the ball down before I release it.

"It's the timing," says Dad. "Do it again."

I do.

And, at Dad's direction, I do it twenty more times.

Dad goes back to the catcher's position.

My wrist is a little sore, but I throw.

"Better," says Dad, which in Dad language means "pretty good."

I throw for what seems like twenty hours, or until Dad says, "Okay."

I wait for him to give me a few drills, but he looks at his watch. "You're getting a lot of good cardio with basketball," he says, "so just give me some crunches and mountain climbers."

"Just," I sigh. Dad said it as if these are easy, which, especially at the end of a tough drill, they are not. But I drop and do them, noticing that the cold ground is harder than it was earlier in the season.

Dad watches me, so it's not like I can sit outside and then go inside in fifteen minutes and say, *Finished!* And sometimes if I get sloppy at the end of a drill, Dad will call me on it and add five more reps. You never really want to do five more mountain climbers, so I make sure to get them done the best I can the first time.

"Nice," says Dad as I finish my last one. He eyes my backpack, which I brought outside. "Anything in there that you need?"

I nod and pull out my basketball and one of those over-the-door hoops that I had at Mom's house. I run up the steps and slip the hoop over the railing of the deck, looking down. There's a small patio underneath the deck, where Dad keeps the trash cans. I run down and slide those over so I can use that concrete area as a court.

Dad nods. "Clever," he says as he watches me line up some shots.

"You don't have a net here!" I say. When we play basketball at Dad's, we usually go to the park down the street, which has a few courts.

"We have great full courts nearby, which are better than just a hoop," says Dad, and this seems to give him an idea. "We could have you run down there, take your shots, then run back."

I give Dad a look. My stomach still hurts from the crunches. "This will work," I say.

Dad shrugs and says, "Get yourself breakfast and get ready. We have to leave in forty-five minutes."

I nod at him and concentrate. The shooting drill

I'm doing is important, but it's not like I can practice passing when I don't have anyone to pass to. Doesn't Dad know this? I sigh. *Sometimes you have to tell people what you need,* says Gary's voice in my head.

But he's my father. Shouldn't he know?

I look up. He's watching me.

"Hey, Dad?" I ask. "Could you help me with some passing?"

"Now?" My dad has the morning routine down to the minute. He does not like it when it's thrown off.

"Well, maybe later," I say.

"Sure," says Dad. "Maybe we can work it in, but right now we're on the clock, kiddo."

He goes inside, and I wonder if he means it. If I had asked him for more work on my curveball, he would have done it right then. I'm annoyed.

He's a freak of a baseball player. Am I a freak? Am I being made into a freak?

I look up as I get into position, and see Dad in the window, watching me. I wonder what he's

inking. Does he feel bad about not helping me? I asked for help. I guess sometimes you can ask and still not get what you ask for.

What I didn't ask for but can't get out of is a newspaper assignment for my media studies class, and that grand assignment is to write about the new outdoor classroom. In theory it's a smart idea: build an area outside where we can have some classes when the weather is decent. I don't like being pent up in the building all day, so I think it's cool, but writing a whole article about it? Not cool. I sit in class, worried that I'm already behind.

We're supposed to write down interview questions and list all the information we need to gather in order to write a story. Then we can go interview one of our sources. Most kids are eager to roam the halls looking for sources, so many of them started interviews right away. I'm set to talk to Mr. Spring, the science teacher who's leading the charge for the new classroom. I realize that, with my deadline, I'd better get going. I pop the

top down on my laptop and raise

I please go interview Mr. Spring?" I

has a few minutes."

"Are you prepared?" Mrs. Tyler asks.

"Absolutely," I lie.

I really have no idea how to be prepared for an interview, since I've never conducted one before. I was interviewed once for a town newspaper, after we won the state championships for baseball. The reporter asked how I felt about the win, and I said, "Great!" And that was what was printed. It wasn't the most thoughtful answer, but then again, what had they thought I was going to say? *Uh, it was okay to win?* Maybe what you ask does matter, and I think about that as I tap on the doorframe to Mr. Spring's classroom.

"Come on in, Marcus," he says.

Mr. Spring is known for wearing a different-colored tie-dyed tie every day. Today he's wearing a purple one, and as I set up my laptop, getting ready to type, I realize that this is a little weird. Usually it's a teacher asking questions, but today

it's flipped. I just hope I can type fast enough to record his answers.

"Actually," I say, "are you okay if I record this on my phone?"

"Sure," he says. "Accuracy is important. And I'll even let you use your phone during the school day to do our interview," he says, and laughs.

I fish it out of my backpack.

"Okay," I say. "So you're heading up the committee to start a new outdoor classroom. Besides just, like, moving some desks to the grass, what is this, and how will it help the school?"

Mr. Spring laughs. "Yeah, it's a little more than moving some desks to the grass," he says. "How do you feel about being cooped up in a classroom?"

"I always look outside?" I say.

"Exactly!" says Mr. Spring. "Outside is generally more interesting. Fresh air is great. And it's a good change in perspective. If you're really working hard on something and it's just not going right, then taking a break from your environment is a good thing."

"Kind of like a vacation?" I ask.

"Yes!" says Mr. Spring. "We get stuck, and sometimes we need to jolt our view to understand the full picture, to be able to get that missing piece."

I nod, taking notes as I record. "Changes view," I write. Maybe this guy knows Gary.

"So you teach science," I say, wondering where this interview is going. I'm not as prepared as I should be. "How did this lead to the idea for the classroom?"

"On a base level," says Mr. Spring, "I believe in learning about the environment. Much of what we cover in science is about the atmosphere, weather, solar events. It's one thing to teach about the cycle of a tree, and another thing to see the tree and touch it."

"What you're saying," I say, "or what I think you're saying, is that it's one thing to learn about something, and another thing to experience it or see it for yourself."

"Exactly," says Mr. Spring. "We miss a lot of things, sitting inside classrooms and offices.

The outdoor classroom is more than just having benches and tables where we can sit outside. It's really an invitation to open your eyes about the world around you. There's nothing like being outdoors to see life close up."

Great quote, I think, my mind on the assignment. Mr. Spring hands me a sheet that outlines the costs for the project and lists the timeline for it.

"That's what was presented to the board of education," he says. "They have to approve it before we break ground."

I glance at it. The paper seems to have all the facts I need to write the story. "Got it," I say. "I think I have everything I need!"

That's the thing. Sometimes when you think you have everything you need . . . you find out you don't.

CHAPTER 9

I'M NOT GOING TO LIE. BASKETBALL
practice this afternoon is rough. Our first game
is coming up, and the team we're set to play is
good. Coach Fuller is really putting us through
the paces and not letting up.

"Pass!" Coach Fuller is screaming from the
sideline. "Pass, pass, pass. I don't want to see anyone running down this court without passing!"

Unfortunately, there are some players who
don't hear that screaming. Like James.

"I have no one to pass to!" yells James.

"You have four other players on the court!" screams Coach Fuller. "Pick one!"

James scowls and passes to Jayden, who makes a beautiful layup.

"That!" says Coach Fuller. "Do more of THAT! This team needs to work as a machine, not as just a few players charging the net!"

He divides us into squads for a scrimmage. "I want to hear you talk," says Coach Fuller. "Talking is important. Signal where you are to your teammates, call out for plays. Communicate. Communication is key. You have to tell people where you are and what you need."

Tell people what you need. For a second I imagine Gary's head on Coach Fuller's body.

Instead of looking down at the court, I talk.

"Jayden!" I yell, and he looks up and passes to me. I take the ball down, knowing I have to pass off. "James, where are you?"

"James, he's asking for you," says Coach Fuller. "Your job is to get down that court and wait for him. Where are you?"

The whole practice goes like that, with us taking turns calling out names. At the end of the practice we're moving tight, and it feels good. Coach calls us all in.

"You are now working like a well-oiled machine," Coach says. "And you look great. I need you to play like that in the game. Bring it in."

We all put our hands into the center and yell, "Warriors!"

As we go into the locker room to get our stuff, I notice Melanie sitting in the bleachers, watching the practice, which is a little weird. Then I spot Mom and wave, hustling in to grab my bag so we can head out.

I meet Mom in the hallway. Sabria is with her. "We have to get a few things for our upcoming trip," says Mom, hurrying out to the car. Sabria rolls her eyes.

"Like what?" I ask.

"Like a new tent, for starters," says Mom. "We need one that we can all sleep in."

Sabria moans. "All three of us in one tent?"

"Yes," says Mom as she drives out of the parking lot. "For one night. You can do it. Or I guess you could sleep outside if you prefer, but that might not be the safest."

"Why?"

"Well," I say, seizing the moment, "there are animals who might try to eat you."

"Marcus!" says Mom. "There might be bears or other animals, but we'll be careful about where we pitch our tent. We'll be fine."

"Bears like to eat pretty girls," I hiss at Sabria, who screams.

Mom stops the car in the shopping center lot. "Can everyone just help me with this?"

We follow her into the camping store. Mom has a list, and the salesperson helps her gather stuff, like a tarp, extra flashlights, and a radio. She also puts a pretty big first aid kit into the cart.

"Most people don't know what to do with most of the stuff in that kit," says the salesperson.

"I'm a nurse," says Mom.

"Then I guess you do," he says, chuckling.

As he packs everything except the tent into a bag, he says, "Enjoy your trip. There's nothing like being outdoors to see life close up."

Where did I hear that before? I wonder if Mr. Spring works at that store.

We drive home, and Sabria and I start our homework as Mom starts dinner.

"Set your phones to silent," says Mom, and Sabria and I both put our phones on the counter. Mom and Dad are killer-strict about our phones. The phones can be on after school, but we have to put them on Do Not Disturb at meals, during homework, and at bedtime. Mom and Dad have controls on the phones to read our messages and turn them off after ten p.m. I don't really mind and am just happy I have a phone in the first place.

I know my phone is probably lighting up with a few messages—probably from Robbie and Kai— but I try to ignore them and just churn out the newspaper article. I figure I can write it pretty fast.

"Mom," I say. "I recorded my interview on my phone, so I need it."

Sabria rolls her eyes.

"It's source material," I say, trying to use impressive words I learned in class. I ignore the texts that are popping up, and replay the interview. Then I look at the fact sheet Mr. Spring handed me.

I start to write about the timeline and how much the project will cost. Who knew it could cost thousands of dollars to put some wooden benches and tables on the grass? Then I scan down to see that the area needs to be prepped. There's an asterisk, and I look at the bottom of the page. "Much of the prep will be done by students." Huh. Mr. Spring didn't mention that.

There's another paragraph about seasonal maintenance. Over the summer the outdoor classroom will be maintained by a volunteer staff. *Who is going to volunteer?* I wonder. I shrug. "The matter of who will volunteer is not specified in the plan," I write. That's correct. I guess that can be a follow-up question for Mr. Spring.

I have the whole article pretty much written in under an hour. It wasn't exactly difficult, but I have to shape it so it makes sense. Still, something is missing. It just doesn't seem that interesting. Maybe news isn't supposed to be interesting. If the news is just supposed to arm people with facts, then this article seems to work. I read it again, then insert a quote from Mr. Spring after I play it back from the recording. That helps, because Mr. Spring is pretty passionate about the outdoor classroom. It isn't just a patio at school. It's "a chance for kids to learn in an engaging, ever-changing setting," according to him. That gives me an idea for the headline, too. "A Classroom with No Walls." Cool. It has a ring to it. I have to upload the article and the headline to the site Robbie is managing. I also upload the design that was included in the fact sheet, in case we have room for a picture.

Done.

It might not be front-page news, but it's a good article. I think, *Maybe I should consider baseball, basketball,* and *a career as a reporter.*

CHAPTER 10

THE NEXT MORNING DAD HAS ME BACK ON
curveballs.

"You control the spin," says Dad.

I nod. I know that. The spin is under my control.

Except it isn't coming easily today. "Five senses,"
I say to myself, calling up the game Gary taught
me. "Five things you hear."

Dad's yelling.

A car going by.

A bird.

A door slamming shut.

My breathing.

In through my nose.

Out through my mouth.

I wait a second. Then throw.

"Good!" yells Dad. "That's it. Whatever you're doing to ground yourself, keep doing that!"

Dad doesn't really buy into a lot of the stuff Gary teaches me or Mom reiterates, like the slow, controlled breaths. But he's learning that if it helps me, it's the best thing for me.

Next sense: seeing. Four things I can see.

I see a squirrel stuffing its puffy face with one more acorn before winter sets in.

I see a tree with bright yellow leaves still clinging on.

I look down and see that my left shoe is untied. I lean down to tie it.

I see my dad's eyes, watching me, waiting.

Breathe in. Breathe out. Throw.

Dad nods. "Control that spin!"

I throw a few more.

"Control, control, control!" says Dad. "Control what you can!"

After we finish, I grab my basketball. The hoop on the deck works, but now it's a little slanted. I run up the stairs and try to straighten it, but it isn't lying flat.

Dad follows me up the steps. I'm irritated that it won't lie straight, so I pound it a bit.

"Whoa," says Dad. "Don't damage the deck."

He leans over, pressing his weight on the part that's sticking up.

I stomp back down the stairs, angry. Instead of shooting, I just do some dribbling drills, which Dad is watching. I set the timer on my phone, then go at it.

Block it out, I hear Gary say in my head. *Center yourself. Breathe in and out.* I do all that.

Then I hear, *Know what you believe.* I believe I'm a good basketball player.

Bounce, bounce, bounce. "I believe I'm a good basketball player," I say softly. I shoot the ball.

"I'm a good basketball player," I say again, a little louder, and dunk.

When the timer goes off, I feel good. It was an intense practice, and I felt my timing improve. When I look up after gathering my ball and phone, Dad has already gone inside.

"News is always of interest," says Mrs. Tyler, holding up the local newspaper.

We all lean forward to see what she's talking about.

"Remember the story about the fire we read?"

"The one with the discrepancy between the fire being suspicious or just under investigation?" asks Sara.

"That one!" says Mrs. Tyler excitedly. "Someone read me this headline and story." She tosses the paper to Oscar.

"'Wiring Affects Warehouse' is the headline," says Oscar. "Yesterday the fire chief of Medford confirmed that frayed wiring was the reason for the fire that burned down the Command Warehouse, which stored mostly building materials. The warehouse was constructed in 1980, and wiring hadn't been updated. While the wiring had passed the initial inspection, having the wiring up to current code could have possibly prevented the extent of the fire. Nothing inside the warehouse was salvaged."

"So what do we know now?" asks Mrs. Tyler.

"There's nothing suspicious," says Robbie. "It was basically a giant accident."

"Seems like it, right?" asks Mrs. Tyler.

"So why did one article say it was suspicious?" I ask.

"Good question," says Mrs. Tyler. "Were there motives for adding that detail?"

"Maybe to get people to read the article, or wait for a follow-up story," says Oscar.

"Or to make it more dramatic," says Sam.

"Or maybe the reporter didn't actually know," says Sara. "Under the law, most fires are suspicious until the reason it started is confirmed. At least that's what my uncle says."

"Was the article trying to stir something up?" asks Mrs. Tyler.

"Maybe not," says Sara. "Maybe the reporter went by the official paperwork, which would list it as under investigation until the investigation is concluded."

"Even so," says Mrs. Tyler. "What we took away from the article wasn't necessarily what was intended. We interpreted the article to mean that there might have been some illegal activity. But the article probably stated the official description of the investigation. Words matter. Let me say that again: words matter. Be careful of the words you're choosing when you write your articles, okay?"

Most of the articles are due this week, with some of them coming in after matches or games are played. Everyone is kind of excited about publishing the paper. My article isn't necessarily the most exciting thing, but I'm proud that it has a lot of facts and information in it, in case anyone is curious about how much is involved in saying, *Okay, class, let's head outside.*

"A reminder that the *Warrior Writes* is out today," says Mrs. Tyler, "so it's a good idea to see what they're covering too."

I grab a copy of the *Warrior Writes* at lunch, and Kai and Robbie and I all take a look.

"Hey!" says Kai. "Read this!"

I look at the page he's pointing to. "The boys' basketball team is set for a great season, says Coach Fuller," Kai reads. "I have tremendous talent on this team, including Marcus Stroman, who is one of the best defensive players we've had in years. He's a strong anchor of this team."

"Whoa," says Robbie.

"Whoa," I say. I had no idea Coach Fuller thought that highly of me.

"Well, he says nice things about James and Jayden, too," says Robbie, and he begins reading aloud farther down. "I have to say we have a great team. They all play well together, and you can really see the chemistry on the court. They work to get that ball into the basket. I'm very excited about what I think will be an incredible season."

"Wow," says Kai. "It's a good thing when a coach sees great things ahead for a team."

I look around the lunchroom as kids are flipping through the paper. I wonder how many of them are reading the story.

I think of what Dad tells me about being called a great baseball player. "You take it in and savor it, but you keep your head down," he says. "No gloating."

I understand not gloating. Nobody likes that, but if I work hard and the praise is earned, I can still celebrate it.

I find out how many kids are reading the story when I get up to throw out my trash. Miles jumps in front of me and yells, "Mr. Basketball, don't block me from the trash can!"

I laugh but take note. People definitely notice what's written about you.

CHAPTER 11

THEN IT'S GAME DAY. IN THE LOCKER ROOM
before the first game of the season, Coach Fuller
gives us a pep talk.

"This is a team that plays as a team," he says.
"That is important. This is not an individual
sport. You rely on and lean on each other on
the court. Respect each other, look out for each
other, and play like a team. Bring your best."

We're all used to this kind of pep talk, but it
always gets us excited anyway. We pump our fists

and are amped to run onto the court. I sprint out, eager to get started.

I look up and see Mom, Dad, and Sabria in the bleachers, and a lot of kids from school have come too. Kai and Robbie are just behind the bench.

Warm-ups are a blur, and before I know it, the clock is running and we're in the game.

We dominate in the first half. We shoot, block, and batter. The other team is as good as expected, but we hold our own. There's some trash-talking on the court, but nothing terrible, even though a kid from the other team says, "Hey, maybe stay on the mound and off the court."

I just swipe the ball from him and say, "I'm good on both."

Our team plays together, as Coach Fuller told us to, with us talking and passing. "Marcus!" I hear as I yell, "Jayden!" We're running the plays as planned. Nothing is going wrong. The fact that we come out so strong seems to surprise the other team, which isn't playing up to the level of their hype.

At halftime Coach Fuller shows us some plays and tells us not to let up. "There's still another half. Remember that. There is still half a game to go. Do. Not. Let. Up."

Maybe we don't hear that part. Or maybe we try our best and it just isn't good enough to combat the other team, because the second half is not like the first half at all. The opposing team comes out hard, determined to wrestle away our lead, which keeps shrinking, basket after basket. Worse, they have a guy who seems to be making every impossible three-point shot.

We, as I hear from the crowd, can't make a basket. Which is true. No shots are going in. Even Jayden, who is under the net, is getting blocked or is missing the basket. James misses free throws, which he never does. It's like everything is going down the drain.

I can say I play hard, which I do. I can say I try, which I do. I can say there probably isn't much I can do and that sometimes games just go in a different way than you think they will, and you lose. All of that is true. But then it comes down to the fact that with five seconds left in the game, the other team throws an impossible three-pointer and makes the shot, burying us with a solid lead.

The buzzer ending the game is a horrible sound, and the whole gym lets out an anguished "Aaaarrrgggh" as the other team celebrates their win, which seemed to happen in slow motion.

To make matters worse, on my way off the court, Melanie yells, "Hey, Marcus, how do you think the game went?"

I look at her like, *Are you really asking me this question?* and stop for a minute. "Great," I say with sarcasm, with the voice I would use if someone asked if I was really excited about thirty-six hours of homework. "Just great."

The locker room is quiet as we sit on the benches, wondering what went wrong. Some lockers are slammed shut as sweatshirts are thrown on and sneakers are stuffed into bags.

Coach Fuller comes in and calls us over. "Here's

the thing," he says. "Sometimes you lose because you play badly. But you did not play badly. You played well. You played as we've been training to play. But that team really had it together. They had better baskets and a kid who could hit a three-pointer from any place on the court, and that made the difference. But as a first game, I'm thrilled at your performance. I'm proud to be your coach. That was the number one team in the county, and we just sent a message that we are coming in hot on their tail. Let's take this as a good first game and move on. There's a whole season ahead of us."

You can tell I'm not the only one who's skeptical about this.

"Rejoice at a loss," mutters James. "That's a new one."

Jayden shrugs. "We played a good game," he says. "Sometimes that's how it rolls."

I hate losing, but it isn't realistic to think you'll win every game. Some matter more. Some you have a better shot at, but everyone says that you shouldn't let one loss trounce you. I can say that. Sometimes I don't totally believe it, though.

The next morning Dad is waiting for baseball practice, as usual.

"You are a heck of a ballplayer," he says, smiling.

"Thanks," I say.

"I mean basketball," Dad says.

I look up. "You mean that?"

"Do I lie to you?" asks Dad.

I laugh. "No," I say. "But we lost."

Dad shrugs. "Yeah, sometimes that happens. But you didn't lose because you didn't play well. You lost because the other team was better at shots and a little more disciplined. You guys are going to go far this season."

Then he walks over and crouches down, holding up his glove.

I throw.

But my mind isn't in it.

"Control the spin!" Dad calls.

My thoughts are spinning. Is he telling me I'm good at basketball just to make me feel better for losing?

I try to center myself. I try to breathe deeply. But I'm just getting worked up and throwing wildly.

"Whoa!" Dad yells as I come a little close to winging one at his head.

He sits back and looks at me. "Okay, let's move on to core," he says.

I run around the cones. I do mountain climbers. I do push-ups and sit-ups. Then I do planks.

It should wear me out, but all it does is heat me up.

I stomp around the yard, putting the cones and balls back into the shed.

Then I huff over to pick up my basketball. We're at Mom's house, so I slam the gate, go into the driveway, and bang away at shots.

"Marcus," says Dad, standing nearby. "I know you don't like losing. But don't lose focus."

"You mean don't lose focus on baseball, right?" I ask.

"Yes," he says. "Don't let losing a basketball game take away your focus on baseball practice."

"Why?" I yell, chucking the ball at the garage door. Dad eyes the door, where there's now a scuff mark.

"What do you mean, why?" he asks. "Because you have a real shot at baseball, a shot at becoming a pro. You can't get distracted."

"I am not distracted!" I scream, loud enough that Mom opens the front door and steps out.

"Our son is upset about his game last night," says Dad by way of explanation.

"'Our son is upset about the game'?" I yell. "Of course I'm upset about the game. We lost. I lost! But it's not about the game!"

"What is this about, then?" asks Mom.

"It's about you not supporting me playing basketball," I say. I instantly felt better after I say that.

"Of course we support you," says Mom, looking confused.

"Well, yes, if it's not getting in the way of or

conflicting with baseball," I answer. "Everyone just sees me as a baseball player. Maybe I can be both. Maybe I can be a baseball player and a basketball player and a football player. And a tennis player!"

"That's a lot of practices," says Mom.

I look at her.

"Okay," she says. "No one is saying you can't also be a tremendous basketball player. Or an all-around athlete."

"He is," I say, practically spitting my words at Dad. "He doesn't care about basketball."

"That's not true, son," says Dad. "What have I done to make you think that?"

"You make me get out here every day and train for baseball. When I added basketball training, it was like, 'Oh, that's cute.'"

Dad opens his mouth, then thinks about what he's going to say.

"That wasn't my intention. I thought you were fully focused on baseball and while you liked basketball, it wasn't as important to you," he says.

"Well, it is!" I say. "I hate being classified as *just* a baseball player. I am more than that. I can be more than that."

We're all quiet.

Mom rubs her head. "We are listening to you, Marcus," she says. "I need you to understand that we are listening. We don't always get it right, but we are trying to listen and trying to give you what you need."

"Clearly we need to make some changes," says Dad. "But let's all process this a little."

I try to process it all day.

But I keep getting angry.

I'm still stewing at lunch when Kai says, "What is going on with you?"

"I lost a game," I say. "You know how I get."

"I know how you get," says Kai, "which is why I'm asking you what's wrong. You are never happy to lose, but you're usually angry when you make a big mistake or don't play well. You played well last night. You didn't make a big mistake. So what gives?"

"Is it because basketball is a new sport?" asks Robbie.

"Basketball isn't a new sport!" I say, exasperated. "I've always played basketball. Maybe not at the level that I play baseball, but now I'm on the middle school team. A lot of kids got cut. I didn't."

"Whoa," says Kai. "Hold up there."

"I got cut," says Robbie. "I'm one of those kids."

He's right. He was cut. I give him props for trying out, but he isn't a great basketball player.

"I'm not as good as you," says Robbie. "It's a fact. It's okay. But don't act like you're the only one who gets disappointed."

"I think Marcus is talking about feeling something different," says Kai.

"I am," I say. "I understand disappointment. And I'm disappointed that you didn't make the team too. But right now I'm upset that people just see me as a baseball player and nothing else."

"Who thinks that?" asks Robbie.

"Everyone!" I say.

"So you don't want to be known as a great

baseball player with pro potential? You just want to be great at everything?" Kai asks. "I'm trying to figure this out."

"I want to be respected," I say. "I want to be seen as the kid who can kill it on the basketball court and the baseball field. There are plenty of athletes who play multiple sports. Why can't I be one of them?"

The three of us sit there quietly.

"Okay," says Robbie. "You're a great basketball player."

"You definitely are," says Kai.

We sit there for a few minutes not saying anything else, just chewing and thinking.

"For the record, I think you'd also be great at water polo," says Robbie.

"Oh, but maybe more synchronized swimming," says Kai, playing along.

"Fencing," I say. "You know I could kill it at fencing. It looks wild. I mean, you're swinging swords around."

"Dude, you probably could," Robbie says, laughing.

"Don't skydive," says Kai. "You could break too many things that might affect the other sports."

I laugh for the first time all day, which I appreciate as much as I do the great friends who can pull me out of just about anything.

CHAPTER 12

AFTER LUNCH I FEEL THE FIRST BIT OF
relief. I also have to laugh as I pack up my locker
at the end of the day, because Kai and Robbie are
pantomiming a synchronized swimming routine
in the hall, while singing.

"Join us," sings Robbie. "Join us as the captain
of our team!"

We don't have basketball practice after school,
and we're headed for a three-day weekend, so
I'm looking forward to that, even if it means a
camping trip with Mom and Sabria in the middle

of nowhere. Since my mind is on other things, that's probably why I totally forget that the *Warrior Times*, the media studies newspaper, is publishing today. And I don't think I have much to worry about.

Until my phone starts buzzing. And buzzing.

Robbie and Kai reach for their phones as I load up my backpack. Then they look at me.

"What?" I ask, looking down at my phone.

Message after message pours in.

You okay?

She doesn't understand sports. At all.

Why in the world did they let her write that?

"What is this?" I ask.

I see Robbie gulp. "It's the *Warrior Times*," he says.

I see the link in the classroom app and hit it. The lead story is about the new teacher. The next story is mine, which looks pretty good as I scan it.

Then I see that the stories have comments listed under them.

"There's a comment section?" I ask.

"There's not supposed to be," says Robbie, who looks like he's going to throw up. "It must have been in the template and I forgot to turn off the option."

Comments are piling in on every story. I look at mine. Some kids are already saying that the outdoor classroom is too much work, and that we're going to have to mow the lawn to maintain it.

"Okay, these comments are ridiculous."

Kai and Robbie look at each other.

"Marcus," says Kai. "There's a story about basketball."

My finger swipes through until I see it. There it is. And I feel like someone has punched me in the gut.

The headline:

THIS IS NOT STRO'S SHOW:

WARRIORS LOSE FIRST GAME.

"No," I say, sliding down to the floor as I read the article.

Marcus Stroman, backbone of the Warriors baseball program, strutted onto the court Thursday night but couldn't do what he does on the mound: deliver a mind-blowing performance that holds up the team.

"Who wrote this?" I cry, scrolling back up. Then I see the name. "You have to be kidding me."

Melanie.

"What does she have against me? And what does she know about basketball?"

"Hang on," says Robbie, pulling out his computer. "Hang on, and I can fix some of this."

He sits on the floor next to me as I watch the comments rolling in on my phone screen. He types a few things into his computer and starts to pull his hair, like he does when he's really rattled.

Stro should stay on the mound.

Stroman needs cleats, not sneaks.

Stro, you need to go.

Stroman should have had more fouls called on him.

Comments are coming in fast.

He thinks he's a premier athlete. He's not.

He's way too short to play this game.

He's totally short. Shortie stay home!

My stomach sinks further and further down.

"What are you doing, Robbie?" asks Kai.

"Disabling the comments," says Robbie, frantically punching his keyboard.

He's not even going to make the majors for baseball. Give it up!

Get a hobby, not a new sport, Stroman.

Go back to the bullpen.

We hear the clicking of high heels in the hallway and look up, not realizing all the kids have cleared out already.

Mrs. Tyler is walking quickly down the hall.

"Robbie!" she calls out. "We didn't discuss the comment section!"

"I know," he says. "I didn't realize it was enabled. I just shut it down."

"Can you erase what's there already?" asks Mrs. Tyler, looking really worried.

"I think so," says Robbie, pulling more at his hair.
I scroll more.

He thinks he's great. Nice to see him taken down.

Ouch.

"There," says Robbie. "There, I did it. I deleted
them."

The comments I'm reading disappear.

"Okay, future comments are disabled, and I
erased the ones that were there," Robbie says. He
looks relieved, and so does Mrs. Tyler.

"Thankfully," says Mrs. Tyler. "Okay, this is all
going to be a great lesson and discussion next
week."

She clicks away toward the office, probably to
explain to someone what happened.

I lean against my locker. The comments are
gone—even though they're still blasted onto my
eyeballs—but the article is still up.

"If you keep reading the article," says Kai, "she
actually compliments you. She says you're part of
a 'strong team that shows great skill and great
promise.'"

"She says that after she pretty much tells me to go back to the bullpen?" I ask.

"Well, that was someone in the comment section. As for Melanie's article, you could read it a few ways," says Kai. "The question is what she really intended here."

"What does she even know about basketball?" I ask. "What made her qualified to write that story?"

"Were you not paying attention in class?" asks Robbie. "Her dad is an assistant coach for the Knicks. That whole family is all about basketball. She knows the sport."

I guess I tuned that out.

"Knowing the sport doesn't mean she's a great sports critic," says Kai. "And it definitely doesn't mean she's a nice person."

"Not after that quote," says Robbie.

"What quote?" I ask, rereading the article.

Melanie wrote, "On the way to the locker room, Stroman, when asked how he felt the game had gone, said, 'Great.'"

"ARE YOU KIDDING ME? I said 'great' like, 'Oh

yeah, it was exactly what we wanted, to lose.' I did not mean the game was great!"

"Yeah, that definitely didn't sound like you," says Robbie.

I put my head into my hands.

The hallway is quiet, and I realize my mom is probably freaking out in the parking lot, waiting for me as school empties out. I stand up slowly.

"My mom is out there waiting," I say numbly.

"I think we missed the bus," says Kai, looking up.

"She can drive us all home," I say.

The Three Musketeers all zip up bags and shuffle to the pickup line, where Mom is standing outside her car.

"Oh, there you are!" she calls. "I figured you forgot something you'd need over the long weekend!"

Then she sees my face. "What happened?"

"We'll explain in the car," says Robbie. "Can you give us a ride home?"

"Of course," says Mom, and we all dive into the car.

"Are you upset about the article?" asks Sabria, even before saying hello.

"What article?" asks Mom.

"The one from the student newspaper," says Sabria.

"How did you get that?" asks Robbie.

"It's posted," says Sabria.

"It IS?" I cry.

"What article?" asks Mom, a little louder. Sabria hands Mom her phone.

I see Mom's eyes get a little bigger, and her mouth twitches.

"This is a little harsh, but it does say your team shows great promise," says Mom.

"Way to try to spin that, Mom," says Sabria.

"Marcus, are you upset?" Mom asks.

"No, I'm totally thrilled, Mom. I love being called out as a poser, especially in the school newspaper. And I love being misquoted that I thought the game was dreamy."

"Attitude, please," she says as she drives down the street.

"The article isn't terrible," says Kai. "It has a little snip in it, but that's all Melanie. The rest is pretty fair and complimentary."

"That's like saying, 'You suck but I like your shirt,'" I say.

"No, it's not that," says Kai. "Let me read this part. Melanie writes, 'Stroman consistently blocked a player known for getting down the court. His ability to press was excellent, and with his lead the team shows signs that this defense is one to be reckoned with.'"

"So you really have to read the whole article," says Robbie, "not just the headline."

I didn't read the full article. "How many people read anything beyond a headline?" I ask wearily.

"That's true," says Sabria, and Mom gives her a look. "What?" Sabria asks. "It's totally true."

"And that quote from me is out of context," I say. "I didn't even really register that Melanie was at the game. She shouted on my way to the locker room, 'How do you think the game went?' And I rolled my eyes and said, 'Great.' I mean, that is not a quote on how we played. It definitely was not meant as a quote!"

We're all quiet on the drive home.

This has the makings of a very *long* long weekend.

CHAPTER 13

MOM LETS US ORDER IN FOR DINNER, which she rarely does. Just to see if I can push it, I ask for a milkshake, and she doesn't even tell me that a milkshake is dessert, which she usually does.

"Do you think talking to Gary might help?" she asks me.

"Maybe," I say, so Mom sets up a call, and Gary calls me before dinner.

"I hear someone's opinion was a little rough today," says Gary. "Why don't you tell me what happened?"

"Well, this know-it-all named Melanie decided to cover the basketball game last night," I say.

"First off," says Gary, "how was the game?"

"We lost," I say. "It was a tough game, but the thing is, we did play well. I'm not too happy that we didn't win, but I couldn't get too upset because we tried and played hard. I'm just mad about other things."

"What things?"

"Well, everyone treated it as 'Oh, Marcus lost a basketball game, but that's just a hobby,'" I say. "Nobody thinks I care about anything besides baseball."

"Do you?" asks Gary.

"Yes!" I say, a little heated. "You of all people should know that!"

"Just checking facts here," says Gary.

I blow out my breath slowly.

"Good breathing," says Gary.

"Okay," I say. "So the article started off with a headline that threw me and seems to be what got everyone's attention."

"What was the headline?" asks Gary.

"'This Is Not Stro's Show: Warriors Lose First Game.'"

"Hmm," says Gary. "Can you read me some of the article?"

I sigh. "Sure, why not read some of the highlights again."

Marcus Stroman, backbone of the Warriors baseball program, strutted onto the court Thursday night but couldn't do what he does on the mound: deliver a mind-blowing performance that holds up the team.

The Lions came to play, and play they did, with an efficient squad that could move the ball up the court proficiently. While their defense wasn't as strong in the first half, it came on in full force in the second, with the experienced squad not only blocking but picking up the shots

they're known for, especially three-
pointers from Lions team captain
Will Chambers.

"With the exception of the headline, this isn't
really opinionated," says Gary.

"Just wait," I say. "A little after that, she
writes . . ."

The Warriors came out stronger
than anyone had anticipated,
playing like a well-oiled team,
looking like they had much more
experience than they actually have.

Where the Warriors failed was
in the second half, when they lost
the zone and couldn't score, despite
repeated tries at the basket. While
Stroman consistently blocked a
player known for getting down
the court, his zone defense wasn't
strong enough, and the Lions, as

they are known to do, found the
holes. Nevertheless, defense for
the Warriors is one to be reckoned
with and one that other teams
will be watching after this first
performance.

"Here's the good part," I say, emphasizing the word "good."

On the way to the locker room,
Stroman, when asked how he felt
the game had gone, said, "Great."
So there's much optimism that this
team will do well this season.

I stop reading and sigh. "I don't think I need to read you the entire thing."

"Okay, but what are you thinking?" asks Gary.

"Well," I say. "While there's some truth in this article, the headline totally blames me. And the first sentence has me strutting out? I mean, what is that all about? And of course I was misquoted."

"Strutting seems a little out of sync with what you'd actually do," Gary agrees. "Does this person know you?"

"Barely," I say. "She's a girl in my class. Apparently, her dad is a coach with the Knicks."

"Ah," says Gary. "It's still odd that she'd call you out. What did you say her last name is?"

"Bradford," I say.

"Bradford?" asks Gary. "Oh. Okay. Yep, coach for the Knicks. Used to be a star college player too, as was his dad, I believe. And I think this coach has a daughter who is a pretty spectacular player?"

"I don't think Melanie plays. Must be her sister. But does that matter? Does that mean she has some cred, so she can shred me like that?"

"No," says Gary. "I'm just trying to put pieces together here to see what her background and perspective is."

"Should that matter? If you're writing about a person, should that make a difference?"

"No, it definitely should not. I'm assuming she just didn't interpret your response correctly."

"But she's not supposed to interpret. I didn't interpret. I reported the facts."

"How did your story come out?"

"It's good, I think. A little boring, but it wasn't meant to be something that makes you think. It was reporting the facts. It had some out-there comments but nothing too over the top."

"Comments?" asks Gary.

I sigh. "Well, Robbie accidentally left the comment section on the site, so kids weighed in."

"Oh," says Gary.

He waits.

"The comments were erased, but I saw them. I saw them on this basketball story. I was called short. I was told basketball is just a hobby. There was one that told me to go back to the bullpen."

Gary sighs. "I'm so sorry, Marcus. That's really rough." He pauses, then asks, "Was *any* of the article accurate?"

I think for a second.

"Did I block well? Yes. Did we kind of crumble in the second half? Absolutely. But why is she saying I should be the one to bring this team to success, based on what I do on a baseball field?"

"That's unfair, I think."

"Yes!" I yell. "That's what I'm saying. Baseball has nothing to do with basketball!"

"It's off, to be sure," says Gary. "Basically she's saying, 'Here's this star player from another sport who everyone is looking to for direction in this sport.'"

I pause. "That's a nicer way to put it."

"Yes, absolutely," says Gary. "Do you want to look at the nicer version of this, or be angry about the hard hits she decided to throw?"

"Is that a choice?" I ask.

"Yes," says Gary. "This is where we're headed. You will see things written about you that aren't really fair. That's bound to happen on social media, especially in sports coverage. And you can seethe, and you can stew. And you will, understandably. You're human. But you can also take the pieces that compliment you and savor them instead. I'm not saying only hear good stuff. I'm not saying just stay happy when someone comes for you. But it's up to you how to spin this. You have control over how you process this."

"So I just hear good stuff and sing 'lalalala' when I read the bad stuff?"

"No," says Gary. "What I'm saying is that you can decide how you react moving forward. The instant sting or hurt? That's real. That happens and you process it. But then you can decide how much sticks and how much you shake off. You could also ignore it altogether. I have professional players who won't even read sports coverage about themselves."

"So what you're saying is that I decide what all of this means?"

"What it means to *you*, yes," says Gary. "You can let the criticism sink in and then deal with it. You can deflect it altogether. Or you can let it sting a bit, as any human would, then choose to say, 'Okay, that's one person's opinion' and just keep going."

I sit with that for a minute.

"What if they're right?" I ask softly. "What if they say I didn't play well and I really didn't?"

"Then are they telling you something you don't already know?"

"No," I say. "I know when I don't play well."

"Then I'd suggest that you block out as much of that as you can. They aren't telling you anything insightful or helpful."

"So hang on to helpful. Hurl the hurtful," I say.

"Something like that," says Gary. "I like the ring of that. Hang on to helpful. Hurl the hurtful."

"Isn't there a way to stop it?" I ask.

"Ah," says Gary. "Unfortunately, no. You can't stop people from believing or saying certain things. And these days we have a lot of ways to voice our opinions and feelings. We can't turn it all off. But you can shield yourself."

I sit quietly with that.

"Can I suggest something?" asks Gary.

"Sure," I say. At this point I need more help.

"You're going camping this weekend, right?"

"I guess that's still happening," I say, sighing. "I will be trapped in a tent with my mother, my sister, and my thoughts."

Gary laughs. "That's not bad! Okay, I want you to do something. I want you to leave your phone at home. Cut it off. Unplug. Tune out. Don't think about basketball or baseball or the games, coaches, viewers, or reporters. Just enjoy being separated from all that stuff. Breathe in some fresh air. Look up. And down, even. Look all around and take in what you see. Listen to quiet or other sounds you don't hear every day. Enjoy the break."

"Okay," I say, not totally convinced that will help.

"When you come back," says Gary, "I'd love to hear what you saw and heard, and what you smelled, even. I'd love to hear all about it."

I smile. "I'll play the Senses game," I say.

"Great idea!" says Gary.

"I have to go," I say. "Dinner was just delivered, and it includes a milkshake."

"A milkshake? Good Lord, you didn't tell me it

was that bad today," Gary jokes, fully knowing that Mom will only okay a milkshake if I'm really upset. "Enjoy the shake, and enjoy the trip!"

I hang up and take a deep breath. Gary is great at making me see that I have choices, that I have some degree of control over things moving forward, which makes me feel a lot better.

Sabria, Mom, and I eat dinner and make a list of who's packing what for the trip. The only thing I contribute are the ingredients for s'mores, which Mom thinks is very funny. After dinner we start to load up the car, and by the time I check my phone before I head upstairs to bed, I have already kind of forgotten about the afternoon. Kind of.

There are a ton of texts.

Nobody listens to mean girls is from Robbie.

Be like Teflon. Let it drip off is from Kai.

There are others, too, including from Jayden:

I'd like to see her try for a three-pointer.

Then there is a text from Coach Fuller, which makes my stomach dip a little. I can ignore it. Or read it and then decide how to react. I take a breath in through my nose and breathe out through my mouth. Slowly. A few times. Then I tap the phone.

All the big athletes know exactly how it feels to have everyone sitting on a sofa criticizing them. Congratulations on making it to the big leagues. In my opinion, you had a great game.

I smile and put the phone down. Then I slide it onto the shelf next to my bed. For now I'm tuning out.

Of course, the next morning Dad is waiting downstairs for a quick workout before we leave. When I come outside, he's helping Mom tie the tent down on top of the car.

He turns to me and opens his arms. Dad's hugs are the best. I have to remind myself that even though I'm older, sometimes I still need a Dad hug, even when he doesn't say anything.

"Let's get this workout in," says Dad, and we head out to the yard.

Dad is watching me intently, but I'm oddly focused. I'm pitching well. It feels good that I'm not letting anything bad in. I'm not letting anything shake me.

"Good spin, son!" calls Dad.

I throw again. Spin is all about control. Controlling the spin requires intent. I think about that.

Dad stands up. "Okay, I won't make you do core right now because you'll be hauling that tent from the car and helping your mother drag all the stuff you need up to that campsite."

"It might be easier to do planks," I say, and Dad chuckles as we walk to the car.

It's pretty loaded down. "Are you moving to the woods, or just going for a night?" Dad asks.

Mom laughs and gets in, and Sabria and I climb in too.

Dad waves, and we pull out of the driveway.

Sabria whips around and gives me a look, and I nod. It's still weird that it isn't the four of us driving away.

I sit back in my seat and look out the window, and soon the town is spinning away as we head out onto the highway. I let out a breath.

"Two hours," says Mom, glancing at the map.

Two hours, I think, *and far away.*

I just hope it feels far enough.

CHAPTER 14

WHEN WE PULL UP TO THE CAMPGROUND, I'm a little disappointed. I don't know what I expected, maybe some grand amazing view or something. It kind of looks like the woods behind Dad's house.

Mom pulls into a parking spot and goes to the office to register while Sabria and I stay with the car. Sabria is frowning. "I don't get reception here!" she says, walking around in circles and holding up her phone.

I'm already getting hungry, so I eye the cooler

in the back of the car and try to wiggle some stuff around to get to it.

"Oh good," says Mom, behind me. "Let's unload and find our spot!"

We unload our backpacks, camp chairs, and sleeping bags. The backpacks are much heavier than I thought they'd be, and I grunt a little as I hoist mine onto my back. Mom pulls out the camping stove and sets up the wagon that we take to the beach, so we can load the groceries, lanterns, chairs, and cooler.

"Team Tent," says Mom, pointing to me and Sabria. I lift it off the top of the car, and Sabria and I balance it between the two of us.

Mom looks into the car and gives a nod. "Okay," she says. "We have everything. Woods, here we come."

We follow Mom up a trail, but stop a few times to put the tent down and rest. We pass a few people at camping spots along the way, some of them families.

"Let's stay a bit close to the trail," says Mom, eyeing a few places ahead of us.

After a few more minutes it seems as if we're the only ones in the woods. Mom sees a clearing and strides over, dragging the wagon behind her. "It looks like we're taking the spot someone cleared out for us," she says.

We lay down the tent. As soon as we do, Mom says, "Let's get that up first so it will be ready when we are."

Sabria and I eye the tent. We've had issues with tents in the past. The last time we camped at the beach, we accidentally poked one of the tent poles through the tent, which wasn't a big deal . . . until it started to rain.

But Mom must have read the instructions beforehand, because she has that thing up fast, and it looks pretty sturdy. Sabria and I crawl inside with our sleeping bags and backpacks.

When we crawl back out, Mom has already hung the bag of groceries from a tree, to keep it away from any animals sniffing around on the ground.

"A bear can still get that," I say, trying to just point something out.

Mom glares at me as Sabria looks like she's getting ready to run back to the car.

"We're smart about things, and bears aren't interested in hurting us," Mom says. She looks around. "It's a fabulously glorious fall day. Let's go take a hike."

We follow her back out to the trail and stay behind her for a bit. The trail is quiet, and all you can hear are the crunching leaves under our feet. Once in a while I kick a rock out of the way to see how far it will go.

Mom is right about it being a beautiful day. The sun is high and bright, and the leaves on the trees are vibrant yellows, reds, and oranges. When the light hits them a certain way, it almost looks like they're beaming light up into the blue sky. The sky is the color blue that I used to use in kindergarten when I colored. I think the crayon was actually called Sky Blue.

We're all quiet, which is nice and peaceful.

After a while Mom says, "Okay, here's the loop we need to pick up," and points to a more narrow trail, going down deeper into the woods.

"Where does that take us?" asks Sabria, peering down the rocky path.

"You'll see," says Mom as she keeps going. "We're going to do this small hike today. Tomorrow we'll do the big hike."

Sabria and I look at each other. This is the small hike? I look behind us, and it seems like we've gone a long way already, but it's probably a good idea to stick with Mom. I shrug and step down. The path isn't that steep, but you have to look where you're going. There are rocks and roots covering the trail, so you have to step carefully. I keep my eye on Mom's red flannel shirt as she keeps walking in front of us. The trail twists a little, and I realize that it's been a while since we saw anyone else. I walk a little faster to stay near Mom. I know she won't get us lost, but I also know that she has a phone in case of emergency.

"Ahhh," Mom says, "there it is."

We look up to see a huge lake spilling out in front of us. There are a few people in the distance, scattered along the rocky trail that goes around the lake. One kid in front of us is on a dirt bike, which looks like fun. I make a note to bring my bike the next time we camp, if we can fit it into the car.

Mom points to her large knapsack and says, "I have lunch, so let's find a spot where we can eat."

We find a big tree stump a little farther around the lake, and Mom unzips her bag and hands out sandwiches and apples. I don't realize how hungry I am until I start eating, and I swallow my sandwich in about three bites.

Mom silently hands me another sandwich. I look up, surprised.

"I know my son," she says, and I smile, eating the next one a little more slowly.

The three of us sit there for what seems like a long time, stomachs full, resting, and watching the lake.

I get up and grab a few stones. Sabria sees me and follows. We used to do this all the time—

skip rocks. Of course, since it's me and Sabria, we always compete to see who can get the rock to skip the most. I have to say, when it comes to skipping rocks, having some pitching skills helps. It's all about how you hold the rock, how you twist it, and how you spin it.

I throw one rock, and it skips pretty far.

"About five hops!" I say.

"Nice one!" calls Mom from the stump.

Sabria throws one right behind me. "And five!" she says. She's always good at skipping rocks.

"Tie score," I say, finding another flat rock and buffing it on my shirt.

I throw it, and it skips three times, splashing along the top of the water before it sinks.

"Stand back, little brother," says Sabria, and she gently throws a rock. It skips twice, then goes down like a sinker.

"Ha!" I say. "I am the king of spin!"

"Oh, are you?" she says.

"I am King Rock Skipper."

"You said you were the king of spin," she says.

"What kind of spin are you going to do on that dumb newspaper story?"

"Spin?" I ask.

"Yes, spin," she says. "How are you going to spin it?"

I grab another rock and throw it.

"I could ignore it," I say.

She nods slowly. "You could."

I think for a minute. "If you don't acknowledge something, you don't acknowledge that it happened. You don't give it any importance."

"True," she says. "But you don't deny it either." She walks a little farther on, looking for more rocks.

I pick up another rock and rub my finger along the smooth underside.

"Things are always spinning," says Sabria. "Sometimes they spin too fast or out of control. You can try to change the direction, but it's hard to stop something that's already spinning. It has a force. I don't want to get into discussing centrifugal force or anything, but let's say that most things start to spin with force. They're set into motion with force. But eventually, if the force weakens, the object will stop spinning."

"So," I say, trying to follow where she's going.

"So even if you don't stop the motion, eventually it slows down on its own. Do you understand what I'm saying?"

"You're telling me to let it go," I say. "To not help it spin more."

"I'm not telling you to do anything. It's your choice. But there are some things you let fly and hope they run out of force. That story was a cheap shot. She probably thought she was being cute with that headline, or she was trying to get attention or something. But you can't let that in. You can't spend your energy fielding every cheap shot. You have to let some of them fly and land quietly far away from you. Like that rock."

She sends a rock clear across the water, skipping at least six times. The rock sinks to the bottom. There's no real splash, no sound, just a few bubbles on top of the lake.

I hear a bird squawk nearby, a long *Ka kaw, ka kaw*, and a few branches rustling. Everything else seems still, including the lake. Even the ripples have faded.

I'm not sure if I want to skip away. I just don't want to be that sinking rock.

CHAPTER 15

MOM STEERS US BACK TO OUR TENT AS THE
sun begins to fall, streaking the sky with pink,
orange, and purple. It's definitely getting colder,
so we light the campfire and pile on some sweatshirts as we start to get ready for dinner. We sit
around the fire as Sabria and I roast hot dogs on
sticks. Things taste better when you make them
at a campout, even though we forgot the ketchup
and I have to eat a plain hot dog. Then we get to
the good part: the s'mores.

As I pop the last one into my mouth, I look up.

The moon is bright, a huge light in the sky. There are a lot of branches, so it isn't a clear, uninterrupted view, but if you look high up at a certain angle, you can see the stars, what looks like a million of them, flickering in the sky. It's quiet. And it's very still.

The sky is now a purply black all around us as the woods settle into the night. Our fire makes a nice glow in our little circle in the forest. I lean back and look up at my view of the moon and the stars. I feel small, like a speck on the big earth as it spins around. Everything else seems far away . . . baseball, basketball, the *Warrior Times*.

I promised Gary I'd do the Senses thing, so I figure it's a good time.

I smell the burning fire, chocolate from the s'mores, crisp air, pine from the trees, and the lingering smell of hot dogs. Pine and hot dogs are a weird combination.

I see the moon, a glowy fire, my mom, and my sister.

I hear the crackling fire, an owl, and a flutter of

----

something that I really hope is another bird and not some scary animal nearby.

I taste marshmallows and the hot chocolate we just made.

I feel the heat from the fire, the warmth from the camping blanket, the log underneath me, and the scratchy camping socks Mom is making me wear, but to narrow it down to one sensation . . . I feel happy. I'm with most of my family, we had a fun, restful day, and I feel far away from everything that puts pressure on me or upsets me. All the problems, all the issues, all the stress . . . none of that is here right now in the woods. I think about what Gary said about disconnecting. I don't feel disconnected from my family, but I feel disconnected from the bad stuff. It feels nice. It feels peaceful. Nothing is spinning. Everything is calm.

We crawl inside the tent, and Mom zips up from the inside as Sabria and I slide into our sleeping bags. After a few minutes I feel something beside me, and I jump.

"It's me," says Sabria, inching next to me. "I'm cold."

"Come together," says Mom as she moves in between us. Sabria and I scoot in on either side of her. The three of us wiggle close. I can hear my mom's and sister's breathing as we all slowly fall asleep in the dark, quiet night.

I'm up early the next morning, awakened by the blazing sun. When I first open my eyes, I'm staring straight at Sabria, which surprises me until I remember where we are. I wisely do not wake Sabria and crawl out to see Mom sitting in a camping chair, reading a book.

"Good morning!" she says.

"Good morning," I say, yawning.

"Should I throw you a ball so you can have your daily workout?" she asks, joking.

"I didn't bring a ball," I say, grinning. "But Dad gave me workout instructions. It's called Workout in the Woods."

"Okay," says Mom, "let's see this."

I drag a long log closer to her chair and point. "Balance is part of my workout," I say, and I hold my arms out and walk up and down the log twenty times.

Mom nods approvingly.

I walk around a bit and find a branch that can work. I jump up, grab it, and do pull-ups.

"Okay, that's impressive," Mom says.

I go back to the log and do a combination of running around it, then jumping over it, side to side, for its entire length. That's kind of hard, and I'm a little winded.

I put them together, and for about twenty minutes I do the balance-beam log, then the pull-ups, then the running and jumping. Mom watches me.

I'm almost done when Sabria comes out of the tent, looks at me, and shakes her head. "You can't go away without doing this?" she asks. "It's not like we're not getting exercise. We walked a few miles yesterday. And Dad isn't here."

"It's different exercise," I say. "I like the switch-up. And now I can tell Dad that I didn't skip a day." It feels good to work out this way. I don't have Dad's eyes on me, judging. I can just work out because it feels good for my body.

"Whatever," says Sabria as she rummages through the cooler. We eat the muffins Mom packed and have some fruit.

"I think we're fueled up," says Mom, stowing a few extra bags of granola to take with us. "Let's get our big hike in."

We grab our water jugs and follow Mom again, this time heading away from the lake, toward a mountain. Mom hums a bit on the trail, and we quietly follow her, stopping to look as she points out things like a deer in the distance, or a really bright tree with leaves lighting up the branches. While Mom is really chatty in the morning, she is equally quiet on walks or hikes, telling us that it's time to quiet our minds and look around, to take in nature.

"Watch this patch," she says, turning around. "It's rocky and a little steep, so plant your feet."

When Mom says "plant your feet," I think of

Dad telling me to do that for a baseball play. Usually I just put one foot in front of the other and walk around, but in sports—including hiking—you need to pay attention to where you're putting your feet, how you're turning them, how you're leaning into them. My feet feel firm today, despite the scratchy hiking socks.

After it seems like we've been climbing forever, Mom turns around with a beaming smile and says, "Well, now let's see if you agree that this was worth it!"

Sabria and I scramble up behind her.

"Whoa," is all I can say for a second. We have reached a small clearing at the top of the mountain, and it feels like we're being swallowed up in the bright blue sky that domes around us. From where we're standing, it's almost like we can reach up and touch it. Birds overhead flap huge wings as they streak by. I don't realize how high up we are until I look down. We see people on the path below us, but they look like little dots. We scan the ground, and Mom points out the lake in the distance that we walked around yesterday, which now looks like a little puddle.

It's quiet. It's calm. And I feel very far away from everything.

"Different perspective, right?" says Mom, smiling at us. We nod. It is definitely different. I feel connected to the spot I'm standing on, but I also feel tiny, like I'm one very small piece of the world around me. It seems like we stand here for hours.

"I really hate to interrupt this beautiful moment," says Mom sheepishly, "but I want to capture it too. Let's take a quick photo." Sabria and I mug for her. Mom has an actual camera, not a phone, that she brings out for vacations or for holidays or celebrations. She snaps a bunch of shots of the great view we have, then puts her camera back into her bag.

After a few minutes Mom sighs. "I could stand here forever," she says, "but it will take us a while to get back down."

Still, none of us move. Even though the planet is spinning, we're still. My mind is still. I take a deep breath in through my nose and breathe out through my mouth. Then I do it again.

"How are you feeling?" Mom asks.

"Peaceful," I say.

"Ah," she says, "that is how the perfect hike should make you feel."

She wraps her arms around us, and we stand for a minute longer, watching the birds fly, the branches below us sway in the breeze, and the choppy water ripple in the lake far below. Things are definitely moving around us, but we're able to stand still. I kind of want to stay like this forever.

Finally we turn around and head back down the mountain, with Mom leading us. I'm a little sad to leave our spot because I know that each step down means we're closer to ending our trip and heading back home. I think about what Gary said about turning things off and really taking a break. I haven't thought about the basketball game in a while. I haven't thought about Melanie's review of my performance in a while. And for a while I haven't thought about the pull between my two sports, or worried about where I should be.

Even though those things are creeping back into my head, on the way down the mountain my feet feel firm. Going downhill is tricky in a few parts, but I feel centered, hearing the crackling leaves and pebbles crunch as we start to see more people in the woods. The farther down we get, the noisier it gets too, with more animal sounds, some chattering from other hikers. I even hear faint music. There are signs all around that we're almost down the mountain, including how far I now feel from the sky itself.

We take our time, and it's a while before we're back at our campsite. The three of us sit on a log to rest as we look at everything that still has to be packed up.

"Packing is the worst part of every trip," says Sabria, and Mom and I nod. We break down the tent, roll our sleeping bags, and fold up the camping chairs. Mom stamps out the spot where our campfire was and, just to make sure, throws a bucket full of water on top. Then we load every-thing back into the wagon. We roll the wagon to the main path and head toward the car. As we walk, the path becomes busier and busier. It's almost a relief to slam shut the car doors and block it all out.

As we head down the highway toward home, things keep popping into my head again, louder and louder. I think about that tough loss. I think about Coach Fuller's speech after the game. I think about how my stomach clenched when I read Melanie's review, and how my stomach flipped when I read the comments below the story.

Then I think about standing on top of the moun-tain, looking out. Gary would tell me to hold on to that feeling. I try, even though as we speed down the road, we're barreling right back toward everything that feels the opposite of peaceful.

CHAPTER 16

IT'S ALREADY DARK BY THE TIME WE NEAR home. Mom flicked on her phone to get a traffic report before we left the campground, but we're quiet on the drive, so we all jump when the phone rings.

"It's Grandma," says Mom, and she taps the phone. "Hi," she says as she's turning off the expressway onto the local highway.

Grandma wants to make sure we're all okay. "I have no idea why you'd go into the woods when you have a perfectly lovely house," she says, and we all laugh.

Grandma is in Florida until the spring, so she goes on and on about how warm it is and about how much she hates winter. When she finally hangs up, we come off the highway into town. As I look around, I realize we're going to pass Dad's house.

I know without saying anything that Sabria and I are both thinking it's still weird to go home and not have Dad there.

"We're close," says Mom to us, maybe sensing it. "Should we swing by so you can say a quick hello to Dad?"

"Probably," says Sabria.

Mom flicks on her turn signal, and as we pull into his driveway, she says, "What in the world is he doing up there?"

Dad is standing on a ladder in front of the garage door, balancing something. He has a flashlight on the ground, pointing up, casting a bunch of confusing shadows.

"Earl, for goodness' sake, be careful!" says Mom, getting out of the car.

"I got it," says Dad, using a drill, which makes a harsh buzzing sound.

"What is that?" I ask, pointing.

"What does it look like?" Dad says, grinning.

"It looks like you're putting something up over the garage door," says Sabria matter-of-factly.

Then I realize what it is. It's a basketball hoop.

"Throw me the net, Marcus," says Dad, holding out his hand.

I find it on the ground and toss it up to him, and he attaches it to the rim.

"We swung by to say hello before we went home," Mom says.

"Well, I wasn't expecting you," says Dad. "I was putting up this rim so it would be ready when I picked Marcus up tomorrow." He throws up his hands. "Surprise!"

I look up at the hoop, a little confused.

"Well," says Dad as he steps down the ladder. "Basketball is important to you, right? You need a net to properly practice basketball. Your defensive rebounds are killing it, but those offensive rebounds need some work."

I feel a lump in my throat. I know Dad is still focused on baseball, but this is a big deal. He heard me. And after a long workday he climbed a ladder in the dark and started drilling the net into the garage, just so it will be ready for me, so he can show me he's listening.

On the way home from camping, the thoughts were coming into my head faster. I tried to block them out, but I'm worried about being able to play two sports. I'm worried that everyone just sees me as a baseball player, nothing else, that I'll always be judged as being this one thing.

And here's Dad, standing in a dark driveway telling me that if I want to go for two things, then I should go for them. He throws me a ball.

I look at it. It's a new basketball, all pumped up and ready to go.

"Figured we'd need one at this house too," says Dad.

I stand there, not really knowing what to do. All I can do is grin.

"Well, player," says Dad, "don't just stand there. Shoot your shot."

I dribble a little, getting my rhythm, then jump. The net swishes as the ball goes in.

I turn around and rush Dad for a huge hug.

And Dad, being Dad, hugs me back but yells, "Don't ever forget about the rebound!" pointing toward the ball, which is now rolling down the driveway.

"Thank you," I whisper into Dad's ear. He hugs me tight.

"If it's important to you, it's important to me," he says, pulling me even tighter.

I run and get the ball, then take one more shot. I see Mom smile at Dad. I know they talked about this. Maybe that's why Mom suggested stopping by. But I kind of don't want to think too much about it. For once I'm relieved when Sabria opens her mouth.

"This is a lovely family moment," says Sabria, "but all of us are in desperate need of showers."

Mom laughs and says, "We really are." We say good night to Dad, and as we pull out, I see him take a shot. He dunks it. I chuckle to myself. Dad is not going to just pass me the ball. He is totally getting ready to play me.

When we finally get home, I feel like we've been away for two weeks, not two days. I unpack my bag and flop onto my bed as Mom yells, "Don't get into those clean beds without taking a shower!"

I roll onto the floor, already hearing Sabria in the bathroom. I look up when I see something flashing, and it takes me a second before I remember that I left my phone at home, per Gary's suggestion.

I grab it and am a little surprised to find 364 messages. For real. Most are in a thread from the other musketeers about how bored they are. There are a few sports scores, and a bunch from other friends checking in on me, making sure I ignore "that really ridiculous article."

I sigh and chuck the phone onto the floor. Just a few hours ago it seemed like I was far away. I wish I could go away again. But at some point I have to come back to things.

I pick up my phone and open the school newspaper. First I read my article. It's pretty good. Maybe I should have asked Mr. Spring more questions. But my story is fair and accurate. Unlike someone else's article.

I don't want to read Melanie's article again, so I click away.

We're supposed to read local news stories to discuss in media studies, so I figure I'll get some homework out of the way. I pop open my laptop and go to the site for the local paper, which Dad tries to get me to read every day. The news stories there are as boring as mine is. A local post office is getting a renovation. There's an upcoming town recycling day. That's when it catches my eye: WARRIORS SEND A SIGNAL.

My stomach drops as I scroll down. But a lot of our town teams are called the Warriors. This article is about the high school boys' basketball team.

> The Warriors had a strong start out of the gate last night, taking on the Stony Brook Bears. While the Warriors' offense looked great, they were unable to topple the strong Bears, ranked in the top ten in the state. After an incredible, fast first quarter, with a score of 8–8, the Warriors couldn't hang on as the Bears took four more baskets by halftime.

Ooof. That is a rough way to go into the second half. I skim down.

> There was pressure on seniors Andrews, Carter, and Jackson to lead the team. With able passing and dogged blocking, they did their best

but failed to overcome the mighty Bears squad. When asked how he thought the team had done, Carter said, "We went down fighting, and that's the best way to go down."

Hmm. Is that really what he said? Or did he say something else, like I did?

The thing is, he probably *did* say that. But when you read it in a news article, the tone is lost. Did he lean in on the word "fighting"? Was he joking around? Unlikely, but still. That's the thing. Technically, I answered, "Great," when Melanie asked me how we'd played. She didn't misquote me. However, she could have added "he said in a sarcastic tone" or something, which would have helped people understand why I was saying that.

I remember what Mrs. Tyler said about us writing our stories: words matter.

And they do. They matter a lot.

I'm thinking about that when my phone dings.

I saw the lights on. Are you home? Robbie is texting me.

Yeah, just got home.

Can you talk?

Sure.

I think he'll just call me, but a few minutes later the doorbell rings.

"You want dinner?" I joke, opening the door.

"Nah," says Robbie. "I can't stay long." He looks at me.

"What's up?" I ask.

"I wanted to say in person that I'm sorry," says Robbie.

I blink. "Okay," I say. "For what?"

"For messing up that template for the class newspaper. For not turning off the comments. That was rough. I know it was rough, and it was my fault. And my mistake hurt my friend. For that I'm sorry."

I look at him for a second. It seems like the kind of very formal apology that my parents would make me say to Sabria.

"Well, you didn't do it on purpose," I say.

"No," says Robbie, "of course not. But my mistake caused a lot of people to post really cruel stuff, and I keep thinking about what your face looked like. It was like someone was punching you."

"It felt like it," I say.

"I can imagine," says Robbie, "and I wanted to punch them back to protect you. I've been thinking about it since Friday. I feel like I failed you as a friend, and I never want to do that again."

Robbie's face looks pained. I know he means it.

"It's okay, Robbie. I know it was a mistake," I say. "I knew you didn't intend that. And honestly, while I didn't love seeing those comments, I knew they were being said. I'm not blind to the fact that when a team loses a game, people feel free to blame everyone."

"Well, with professional athletes, yeah, that happens," says Robbie. "But not middle school kids."

"Why is it any better to gang up on professional athletes?" I ask. "They're trying as hard as anyone else. Or you could argue that they're trying harder. It's their full-time job. And, anyway, they're still people. They have feelings."

Robbie nods. "People just have to watch their words."

"They really do," I say.

Watch your words, I think.

"I wish I could help you spin this," says Robbie.

We're quiet.

"I'm not sure it needs to be spun," I say. "Or I guess the answer is that I don't need to spin this for anyone. I need to spin it for myself. I can challenge it. I can ignore it. Or I can see it and hear it and just process it, then let it spin right off me."

"What are you going to do about Melanie?" Robbie asks.

"Do about her?" I say. "I mean, I don't know how much I can do. Besides, I'm not even that mad at Melanie anymore."

"You aren't?" asks Robbie, his eyes bugging out. "She didn't exactly do right by you."

I shrug. "She said what she thought. What matters here is what I think."

"Wow," says Robbie. "That is really freaking grounded. You can let all that slide?"

"Not that easily," I say. "But I can let it just spin. Eventually it will stop spinning."

"That's a talent," says Robbie.

"Well, maybe someone can write about *that*," I joke.

CHAPTER 17

THE LONG WEEKEND IS BEHIND US. WE had a day to just hang out after the trip, and now it was time to get back to everything. I have baseball practice with Dad at Mom's house. After the drills Dad says, "Okay, now we shoot."

I'm confused for a second until I realize that he means we'll do basketball practice together.

I get the basketball from the shed.

"You need work on your spin," says Dad. "We worked on your spin in baseball. But there's spin on the ball in basketball, too. You aren't making the shots because you need more backspin."

I wait. Dad bounces a few times, then shoots.

"See that?" he says as the ball bounces into the hoop. "It's not just about the throw. It's about the spin. That will help you get the ball into the basket."

I know about spin. Coach Fuller has been working on it with us. I hold the ball like Coach Fuller showed us and like Dad showed me. *Swish.*

"Just like that," says Dad. "Do it again."

I bounce and shoot a few times, making a few baskets.

"Okay, that's going to take some practice, like everything else," says Dad. "But you got it. Now get it into your muscle memory so it's natural."

I take a few more shots.

"Twenty more," says Dad, and I'm startled a bit. "What?" he asks. "You said you wanted to take this seriously, so let's take it seriously."

I hide a grin, wondering what I opened up with this. Dad looks at his watch. I shoot twenty shots. I don't get them all in.

"Better," says Dad. "We'll work on it."

I put the ball back into the shed.

"Dad," I say, then stop.

He waits.

"I don't want to go to school."

Dad seems to be about to say something like, *Oh come on, Marcus, you aren't staying home,* but then he realizes why I'm saying it.

"You hold your head high," he says. "You are a good basketball player, Marcus Stroman. People can throw words at you. People can say whatever they want. But you try hard, you play your best, and you hold your head up. You believe in yourself, and no one can take that away."

I know that what he's saying is right. But actually being able to do that is hard stuff.

He gives me a hug, and I head inside, where Mom has pancakes waiting. They're made exactly how I like them: tons of butter on top, and a little crispy on the edges. I'm quiet as I stuff them down, then clear my plate, shower, and get ready to face the music.

When Mom is dropping me off, she turns around

in the car. "You remember how you felt on the top of that mountain?" she asks.

I do.

"You felt strong and grounded and steady, right?" she says.

I do.

"You stay on top of that mountain," says Mom.

I nod, swallowing hard, and then I open the door.

"I'll try," I say. "Watch out, world, here comes the king of the mountain."

She flashes me a smile.

"Stay steady, King," she says. It's such a Mom thing to say.

But as I step out of the car, I hear her voice again. "Stay steady." I plant my feet firmly and walk up to the front door of the school. My stomach is spinning a little, but my feet are firm. *Okay,* I think. *Stay steady.*

As soon as I walk into school, I notice that Kai is standing there. "You waiting for me?" I joke.

"Yes," he says.

I stop. "Really?"

"Yeah," he says. "That was a tough article, and you caught some wind for it in the comments. I was thinking of you over the weekend. I got your back."

I grin. "Can you get me out of here?"

"No," he says. "But I can walk with you to home-room."

Nobody seems different in the halls. The big sign in the lobby of the school doesn't flash MARCUS STROMAN NEEDS TO GO BACK TO THE BULLPEN.

Maybe everyone has forgotten about it over the long weekend.

Until Mrs. Tyler just has to bring it up within the first thirty seconds of media studies.

"I'd like to talk about our first edition of the newspaper," she says, perching on the corner of a desk. "A lot of hard work went into it, which I appreciated. But we had some issues. First off, there was an unintentional error in loading com-ments for the stories. I'm not discouraging opinions, but we don't intend to allow that feature moving forward."

"Why?" asks Melanie.

It's the first time I look at her today.

"Because anyone can say anything to a screen," says Mrs. Tyler. "Comment sections are filled with things people would never say out loud, let alone to a person standing in front of them."

"But a comment section is a way to discuss things," says Sam.

"It could be," says Mrs. Tyler. "But mostly it's used to hurl one-liners, or insults. That's not productive conversation."

"But most of the comments that were posted were things people *would* say out loud," says Melanie.

The class gets quiet.

"Really?" I hear myself say.

Melanie looks at me, crossing her arms, almost as if she's ready for a fight.

"You'd tell me—as someone suggested in the comment section—to go back to the bullpen?" I say evenly.

"Okay, well, we aren't . . . ," says Mrs. Tyler.

"There were comments," I say, still calmly, "that were just pile-on insults. Maybe you'd tell me to go back to the bullpen. Maybe you'd say I'm too short to play basketball. Maybe you'd tell me to choose another hobby instead of another sport?"

"No," says Melanie. "Those are insults, not commentary on your game."

"I agree," I say. "But those statements were in the comments."

"Okay," says Melanie. "Clearly I wouldn't say those were helpful. But they happen."

"I'd argue that your article helped lead the comments in that direction."

"My article was fair!" she says, a little loudly. "You need to work on shooting."

"That is fair," I say. "I do. And certain other players need to work on defense, or their passing, but they weren't called out. What about the part where you said this whole game was on me? That everyone was looking to me to transform from a great baseball player to a leader on the basketball court?"

It feels like I'm just talking to Melanie. The classroom is the quietest I can remember. Mrs. Tyler looks like she's going to say something, then stops.

"I think that's fair," says Melanie. "You are a great baseball player. People know you as an athlete. There's a level that's expected of you."

"I'm well aware of that," I say. "But there were four other players on the court with me. You didn't rip them the way you ripped me."

Melanie looks startled for a second. "But everyone was watching you," she says. "That's the story, Marcus. The story isn't whether or not we have a winning team. The story that everyone wants to talk about is whether or not the legendary Marcus Stroman can pull it off in another sport."

I blink. "What?"

"That's the angle," says Melanie. "That's the interesting angle of the story. I mean, sure I wanted to report on the opening game, which I did. There was good defense overall, the first half was strong, and the team lost. But the reason a lot of people were there was to see you play."

I look to Robbie for help. He's glaring at Melanie.

Steady, I hear Mom say in my head.

Steady, I repeat to myself.

I think of the view from the top of the mountain. I think of how everything else seemed small and far away. I try to look at Melanie as if I'm looking at her from the top of the mountain trail. As if there is some distance.

The classroom remains still. But it's an uneasy stillness.

"Well, that's an angle," I say. "If you wanted to stir stuff up, I guess you wanted an angle."

"That wasn't the assignment!" Robbie blurts out. "The assignment wasn't to come up with an angle. The assignment was to report the story."

"I did report the story," says Melanie. "There wasn't anything in there that wasn't factual."

"Yes, there was," I say. "I didn't strut onto the court."

"Yes, you did," Melanie replies. "The definition of 'strut' is 'to walk with confidence.'"

We look at each other.

"Okay," I say. "Maybe we have a different under-standing of how the word 'strut' should be used. But then, let's take the fact that my quote wasn't exactly in context. When you asked how I thought the game had gone, first of all, you never told me it was for the newspaper. I didn't know I was on record. And second, I said, 'Great.'" I say it now like I said it after the game, rolling my eyes with exaggeration.

"You said, 'Great,'" she replies, challenging me. "That's what I put in the article."

"But you gave no context to explain that I was exaggerating. That's misleading."

"I don't think so," Melanie answers.

"Difference of opinion, then," I say. "But that's the thing. That's opinion. Not fact."

"You said, 'Great,'" Melanie huffs. "I wrote, 'He said, "Great."' What's the issue?"

I honestly feel like I'm going to punch some-thing.

"Okay," says Mrs. Tyler. "Let's take a time-out

here, okay? Everyone take a deep breath in with me, counting to three." Most kids take a breath in. "Now breathe out for three." Kids breathe out, including Melanie. "Three more times."

All you can hear for a few minutes is people breathing in and out.

Mrs. Tyler seems to take another breath. "So," she begins, "was Melanie's article the only one reporting on the game?"

"I guess we're going to gloss over this," mutters Robbie.

"There was an article in the *Warrior Writes*," says Sara. "It mainly focused on Coach Fuller's interview."

"And what was the tone of that?" asks Mrs. Tyler.

"That the team was strong with several anchors, and it was set up for a good season," says Sara.

"Any callouts for Marcus?" asks Mrs. Tyler.

"Yes," says Sara. "Coach Fuller said he was one of the anchors of the team."

"So we have two articles," says Mrs. Tyler. "What if you only read one of the stories?"

"If you read the *Warrior Times*, you'd think the team is toast if Marcus can't do on the basketball court what he does on the baseball field," says Oscar. Then he turns around and mouths "Sorry" to me.

"And if you read the one in the *Warrior Writes*?" Mrs. Tyler continues.

"You'd believe that it was a good team with a lot of talented anchors," says Robbie, "and that Coach Fuller was excited about a strong season ahead."

"Now what?" asks Mrs. Tyler. "Who do you believe?"

"Both?" asks Michael. "You believe that everyone is looking at and looking to Marcus but that the team is there. It wasn't a bad loss. They were up against the number one team in the county, and they held their own for two quarters. But they are looking at Marcus to lead it through."

"That's a good assessment," says Mrs. Tyler. "Anyone have anything to add?"

"If you combine them," says Sara, "it's a little more even."

"No, it's not," says Robbie, and he slaps his hand down on his desk. Everyone turns to look at him. "Why is everyone doing this to Marcus? Why are you comparing baseball and basketball? Did anyone ever ask Pelé why he wasn't a great tennis player?"

Everyone is rumpling their faces, trying to figure out Robbie's logic on that one.

"Just because you're good at one thing," Robbie continues, "that doesn't mean you'll be great at another. And if you are, we should celebrate it, not compare it. Otherwise it's limiting a person to just one thing. It's labeling and it's limiting."

I clear my throat.

"Robbie is one of my best friends," I say. "He'll stick up for me anytime. And he's upset on my behalf. But I'd like to speak for myself." Then I stop. What am I going to say?

The bell rings.

Nobody moves.

Mrs. Tyler looks at me. "Do you want to speak now, Marcus, or can we continue this conversation tomorrow?"

Suddenly things are spinning.

"Tomorrow," I say, "will be fine."

CHAPTER 18

AT PRACTICE THIS AFTERNOON COACH
Fuller is pushing us on passing. "As a team!" he
yells. "Play as a team!"

We're practicing playing zones. "Player-on-
player" means you take one opponent and stick
with them. When you play "in the zone," you
play in your space, and you play against whatever player comes into your space.

"Marcus, up top!" calls Coach Fuller.

"Of course he's up top," mumbles James.
"Marcus Stroman is always on top."

I pause for a second. The comments in the newspaper were anonymous, but maybe one of them can be attributed to James. That would not surprise me. Then again, James says stuff to me to my face all the time.

I keep my head down during practice and don't say much. I don't joke around. I listen to Coach Fuller and give it my all.

Dad is waiting for me by the bleachers as I sling my backpack over my shoulder.

As I walk to the car, I notice that it's one of those first nights when winter is getting close, when the air has a little bit of a bite to it.

When we pull into the driveway at Dad's house, he sighs. "Your sister," he says, looking at every single window glowing with a yellow light. I know it irritates Dad, but there's something nice about coming home to a house that isn't dark, especially tonight.

Sabria has already set the table, and Dad opens the fridge. "Okay. Tonight . . ." He sighs and trails off. "Anyone want pizza?"

"I do!" I yell.

"Homework first," says Dad. "Let's get that done while the pizza is on its way."

Sabria and I sit at the kitchen table doing our work while Dad reads the newspaper. Sabria hums a little bit, which for once doesn't annoy me. Luckily, neither of us has too much homework, so by the time the pizza gets here, we're ready to relax a little.

Dad opens the box and grabs a slice.

Sabria sighs. "Dad," she says. "We need plates."

Dad shrugs and eats his slice right out of the box.

I follow.

Sabria rolls her eyes and gets a plate for herself.

"Tell me about your days," says Dad.

"Yeah, Marcus," says Sabria. "I hear your media studies class was quite dramatic."

I look at her.

She looks at me and smirks. "Yes," she says. "I do know everything."

"What happened?" asks Dad.

Dad rubs his head as I explain how the conversation went.

He rests his chin in his hands when I'm done. "So," he says, "you need to think about what you'll say to Melanie tomorrow."

"I guess," I say.

"Do you know what you'd like to say?" asks Dad.

"'Shut up'?"

Dad laughs. "You know, Marcus," he says, "that's not such a bad response. Part of what I think you see is that we have to block or deflect criticism sometimes."

"So, he can just tell her to shut up?" asks Sabria.

"No, I would not suggest that," Dad answers. "I think there's a better way to handle it, but the automatic response of 'I'm not listening to you' is a good one. You block out stuff that isn't helpful. If she said, 'You need to work on your shooting,' that might be accurate criticism, but even then you wouldn't have to take it."

"What if the criticism is coming from you?" asks Sabria.

Dad looks at her sideways. "Well," he says. "I'm probably criticizing you with the intent of helping you get better at it, from manners to how you're playing, to learning something. Sometimes people just criticize for the sake of giving their opinion. That's not helpful. Those are two different things."

"So a coach might criticize our form because they want us to correct it, to make us a better player for the team," I say. Dad nods. "And a teacher might criticize our essay because they want us to write better. But a kid who criticizes our haircut might just be being mean about it."

"Yes," says Dad. "That's it exactly. You know who to listen to when it comes to criticism. Me, Mom, your coaches, your teachers. It's people who mean well."

"Melanie didn't mean well," I say. "She wanted to sound smart and authoritative."

"Maybe," says Dad. "We don't really know her

from thinking about the game, to thinking about being a baseball player, then about being a basketball player. I keep hearing Melanie's voice say *Great* in my head.

I breathe in and out a few times and feel calmer.

Bounce, bounce, brick.

Okay, the Senses game.

I see the streetlight. The trees lining the driveway. The light on in Sabria's room. I see the front door, painted shiny black. And I see . . . Dad sitting on the front step.

I didn't hear him come out.

"Steady," he calls.

Steady, I repeat in my head.

I feel my feet on the ground, my toes wiggling in my sneakers. I breathe in and out.

Steady.

My head stops spinning.

I'm in control.

I think about what Dad taught me about the spin on the ball. I move my grip around, feeling the ball differently as it leaves my hands.

motivation. Maybe she loves basketball and was disappointed with the results of the game. Maybe she doesn't like you. Maybe she thought she was being fair. We can't make assumptions."

"If we don't know where her intent was, then we also can't really trust what she says one hundred percent," says Sabria.

"Yes," says Dad. "Sometimes it's good to listen. And sometimes you need to block it. You have to be the one to make that call."

I sigh.

"I'm not going to tell you what to say," says Dad. "But if you want to talk it through, I'm here."

"I can tell you what to say," Sabria offers.

Dad and I both give her a look.

After dinner I throw on a heavy sweatshirt and hat and grab my basketball. I see Dad look up as I go out the front door. It's dark, and I can see my breath in the air.

Bounce, bounce, bounce.

I shoot a few times and miss every time.

I'm frustrated and I can't steady myself. I go

Swish.

After a while my body starts to move without me thinking about it.

Bounce, bounce, swish.

My feet feel firm. I feel steady. Nothing is spinning except the backspin on that ball.

It seems like I'm at it for a long time. I'm getting sweaty, and my arms are getting a little tired. I sink one last basket and sit down on the step next to Dad, catching my breath.

"You look good," says Dad. "You feeling a little better?"

"I still don't know what I'm going to say to Melanie," I say.

"It will come to you," says Dad.

I lean back and look up at the sky. It's different from being outside when we were camping. I don't feel far away from everything. But it's quiet and still. Gary is right. I can't totally cut everything off all the time, but I can have moments when I'm unplugged. I sit next to Dad, and look up at the moon, until I know exactly what I'll say to Melanie.

CHAPTER 19

THE NEXT MORNING DAD AND I ARE UP A little earlier for practice. I bundle up because there's frost on the ground.

"Make sure you warm up that arm," says Dad as we start. I can't help but think that he's worried not just about the weather but about how basketball is affecting my pitching.

But my throws feel good this morning. They're sharp and I feel in control. I'm in a zone.

Dad has me do strength building, and then he says, "Okay, next sport."

I follow him to the front of the house, where he has me dribble and shoot. Then his eyes light up a little as he yells, "And now some Knockout!"

Knockout is a drill you do with two players going up against each other. One player shoots. If they miss, then they run as fast as possible to grab the rebound. The goal is to make as many baskets as possible. It's fast, and it can get competitive, especially if you're playing with my father. He goes hard. And he beats me.

"Whoo-hoo!" he yells, jumping up and down. "The old man still has it!"

"Okay," I say. "I'll get you next time."

"Oh yeah?" asks Dad. "Set that bar, kiddo!"

When he drops me off at school, he says, "Have a great day, Marcus." He looks at me as if he's trying to figure out what to say. I wait, my hand on the handle of the car door.

"Stay steady," he says, looking me in the eyes.

I look back at him. "I'm steady," I say.

He holds my gaze, making sure. Then he gives me a hug and I head out.

Kai and Robbie are on the sidewalk in front of the main entrance.

"You guys waiting for me?"

"Our day can't begin without you," sings Robbie, grinning.

I walk into school knowing I have a friend on either side of me. They know I sent an email to Mrs. Tyler last night with the plan. I don't want to just address Melanie in class. I want to talk to every kid who commented.

Mrs. Tyler catches me in the hallway as I'm headed to class after homeroom. "We're all set, Marcus," she says. Then another teacher calls out to her, and as she turns, Melanie steps next to me.

"Marcus? Can I just tell you something?"

I look at her. She's twisting a bracelet she has on her wrist. I nod to Robbie, who goes inside the classroom.

"My intention wasn't to throw you under the bus with that article," she says. "You played well. You are one of the strongest players on the team. And it's a strong team. But it's your lead that everyone is looking to. If I'd written an article just covering the game, then it would have been a bland story about a middle school team losing a game. People are watching *you*. They want to read about *you*."

"I know they're watching me," I say, "and that's not easy."

"I guess it's not," she says. "I'm not an athlete. I'm not bad at sports, but I'm not in the same league as my grandfather, dad, sister, or even my cousin. They are incredible athletes."

She says this matter-of-factly.

"Anyway," she continues, "that's what everyone says. So my plan is to take my knowledge of basketball and spin it into something else, as a sportswriter. I watch a lot of games. I study the sport. I come prepared."

"Okay," I say. I'm not sure why Melanie is telling me this.

"I just wanted to clarify that I know what I'm talking about," she says.

"Thanks for explaining that to me," I say. "I don't want to get into whether or not you understand the game. Or if your criticism of me is valid or not."

She blinks. "You don't care what is written about you?"

"No. You said I was strong on defense," I say. "I know how to block shots on the court and off."

"You two joining us?" Mrs. Tyler asks, stopping at the doorway. I guess we didn't hear the bell or notice the hallway clearing. We both duck into class.

I don't know if anyone remembers that I had something else to say to Melanie. If they do, no one seems to notice that Mrs. Tyler launches straight in. Our next unit is talking about the various sources for finding news. I try to pay attention, but I think about what Melanie said in the hall. Maybe she has a chip on her shoulder because nobody thinks she's a good enough athlete. Maybe she's trying to prove herself in sports another way. But maybe it isn't a chip. Maybe it's a sadness because she doesn't feel like she can measure up.

I get through the day without any more drama, which is a win. Tonight we have another game, and I'm anxious to get out on the court.

I feel good during warm-ups. I notice the gym filling up. I see Mom and Dad, Sabria, Robbie, and Kai. My team has come out to support me.

I feel loose. I feel steady.

Coach Fuller calls us in. He goes over a few plays, drawing them out for us, then glances at the ref. Time to play. "Play hard. Play as a team," he says, and sends us out.

The crowd is loud. "Defense!" they're shouting. But within a minute or two I don't hear anything but the ball bouncing and my team calling my name to pass. It's like I'm in a tunnel zone.

We're playing well overall. We hold the other team, trading baskets back and forth. The hope for a win is building and building. I start to feel a little pressure but hold steady.

There's a kid on the other team who's been using his mouth all game. "Here's the Stro Show," he said right in the first quarter. "Let's see that glitz."

I block him.

He's pushing and grabbing too, but not going too far. I'm holding my own but don't want to get called on a foul.

I stay focused. Steady.

Then it gets tight.

The score is tied in the fourth quarter. There is one minute left on the clock.

I'm getting around on the court well, pressing hard. I'm grabbing a rebound when I hear my new agitator hiss, "Ooh, don't hurt those hands, Mr. Pitcher."

I come down with the ball, glad that I have my hands firmly on it.

And then I feel his hands on my back pushing me forward. I seem to fall in slow motion, until— *thump*—I land on the floor. The landing doesn't hurt as much as it surprises me. I push myself back up and hear the ref's whistle.

Foul.

Foul called, which means I have two free throws.

I have two free throws, with fifty seconds left

on the clock when the game resumes. I can score two points for the team, putting us ahead. We then just need to keep the other team from scoring for less than a minute, and we can win the game.

I gulp a little bit. Pressure.

All I have to do is make two baskets, just like I'm shooting hoops in the driveway at home.

The teams line up, and I stand at the top of the key. *Just two throws,* I think. *Just shoot.*

The crowd is quiet, and when I bounce the ball, it seems to echo everywhere, as if the gym is empty. I don't look at the faces of the players lined up on either side of me. I don't even glance at Coach Fuller. I squint my eyes at the crowd. I try to imagine myself back on that mountain. My feet feel firm.

Bounce, bounce. I block out where I really am. I'm just in the gym, taking some shots. My hands go where they need to go, and with a great backspin—*bank shot*—I have one in.

I register the cheers but don't react.

One more time, I think.

Dad's right about the spin on the ball. And Gary's right about being able to control how things are spinning. Spinning a ball is intentional. Controlling the spin in life means you have to block, defend, guide. Intentional spin or spin you're a part of can be controlled, diverted, pushed.

I know how to bank this shot. I know how to spin this ball. *Bounce, bounce* . . . and it's in. Just like that I have two points and we're ahead. There are cheers as we set up for the throw-in, knowing that a lot can happen in a game in less than a minute. We block, we pass, and we keep that ball until the buzzer, winning by two points.

I'm not gonna lie.

I feel like I'm king of the mountain.

CHAPTER 20

OUR CLASS ISN'T SET TO TAKE A TURN WITH
the newspaper for another three weeks, so we
haven't been assigned any stories. But after I
emailed her, Mrs. Tyler agreed to let me write an
opinion piece for the next issue. I take my time
with it and read it to Gary when I'm finished.

After a recent article was published,
what I was asked most was how I
was going to spin it. The article went
straight at my performance, saying it

was my responsibility to hold up a team. My answer to how I was going to spin the story surprised everyone—I wasn't.

Things spin. They gain energy when that spinning action is fed, with force or with words. Without any energy to help it, though, spinning will eventually stop.

I choose not to give some of the comments—not only from the article but from the temporary comments section—too much energy. First, as the article stated, I'm great at blocking.

Second, a lot of what gets written or posted isn't what anyone would say to your face. Anyone can post a comment like "Yeah, he was terrible" with any username. They can hide behind a screen while they send negative energy with those posts.

Here's the thing: Would that same person say that to me after a game? And would they be prepared for me to say something back?

As a sports fan as well as an athlete, I get it. I sometimes yell while I watch games on TV. I scream when a player drops a ball or doesn't make a shot. I get mad when my favorite team—or my own team— loses a game.

But as the person getting yelled at here, as a person getting nailed with online comments, I'd like to remind everyone that a player is actually a person. A human being. If you walk around insulting everyone on a constant basis with harsh words, then I suppose that's one thing. If you start every conversation with "Let me first insult you," then you go ahead being you. But if you walk around with the intent of trying to be kind and treat people with respect, no form of media gives you the right to ignore that intent.

We're taught that words matter, and they really do. Use yours fairly, kindly, with compassion, and with intent. There is a person sitting on the other side of what you are throwing out.

There's no need for everyone to agree on everything 100 percent of the time. We won't. But disagreeing doesn't mean that you take anyone else down to prove yourself right. You can say you didn't like my performance on a court, but hurling insults while you do it doesn't make me look worse; it makes you look worse.

For those of you who are looking at comments with stomachs flipping

*or fists clenching, I see you. I have
some very good advice to pass along
to you: Don't let this spin you. Take
what is helpful and hurl what isn't.
Stay steady.*

"You can add 'writing' to the list of things you do well, Marcus," Gary says.

Marcus Stroman, writer. I kind of like the sound of that.

When it's our turn to publish, the comments are off, so I'm not expecting any immediate reactions, but as soon as the link for the issue goes out, just like last time, my phone starts buzzing. At first I don't want to look.

That's RIGHT, man is from Jayden.

Glad you showed everyone what you can do—play ball is from Kai.

You should really become a writer AND a baseball player. Oh, and a basketball player too is from Robbie.

That makes me laugh.

I put my stuff into my backpack as my phone continues to buzz. But this time I'm not panicked. A lot of kids yell, "Nice piece" as I make my way outside to go home.

The sunny glare of this late fall day makes me squint as I search the cars lined up. I see Mom wave just to make sure I see her, but I do. I see my friends, my family, and I see myself. And I feel like my eyes are wide open to what I have to do: stay steady. And with my feet on the ground, nice and firm, I run.

AUTHOR'S NOTE

While some of the things that happen in this story are semi-autobiographical, I really set out to write this book because I wanted to share my core beliefs. As a kid, I worked extremely hard, believed in myself, and wanted to not only become a great baseball player but a well-rounded athlete, student, and person. I did—and still do—struggle with believing in myself, staying steady, and making peace with trying my best. I work on myself every day. Mental and physical health are the real keys to success.

Being a great person and athlete doesn't just come from skill or training; it requires mental work to be happy with yourself and to be the best version of yourself. If you ever feel less than your best self or feel like you need help, there's no shame in talking to your parents, teachers, guidance counselors, or mental-health coaches. You are not alone in your feelings. Believe in yourself. You can do anything.

—Marcus Stroman

ACKNOWLEDGMENTS

I'd like to first give special thanks to my mom and dad. I would not be who I am and where I am today without them—their guidance, love, and nurturing. They gave me the perfect balance of love and support while instilling in me a work ethic that is second to none. They worked tirelessly every day to give me every opportunity, for which I am forever indebted.

My son, Kai, has changed my life, the man I am, and the way I see the world and treat others. I want to create a better world and the best life for him. An important step in doing that is taking the time to learn about and understand others. Every single person has their own hardships and struggles, so let's treat people with empathy and lead with love. That's the world I want to create for Kai.

Shannon Nadj, Kai's mother and my wonderful partner, has been an ear for me throughout this process and life in general. She shows me patience and love every day and teaches that to our beautiful baby boy. I am so grateful to her and lucky to share this life with her.

Special thanks also go to my sister, who was instrumental in my upbringing and present through tough times during our childhood. I am forever thankful and grateful for you.

Mick and Jayden, my stepmother and half brother, have been with me every step of my journey. It has been a true pleasure to watch Jayden grow up and become the man he is today. I know Mick is an integral part of that success. I'm incredibly lucky to have her in my life and a great person in a younger brother.

To Pauline Dhillon, who I met as a young man when I first moved to and debuted in Toronto as a Blue Jay. These were formative years for me, and she immediately gave me shelter and has been one of my brightest guiding lights ever since.

Meghan Whelan has been on this journey with me from the start. She has played many roles for me in our decade together—friend, agent, assistant, manager, you name it. She runs my life, and I don't know where I would be without her.

To the whole team at Simon & Schuster. Thank you for believing in me and for taking an idea and turning it into reality. Your excitement, passion for this book, and hard work have made it the success it is. Together we are bringing the importance of mental health to the forefront and making a safe space for conversations with kids.

Don't miss where it all started!

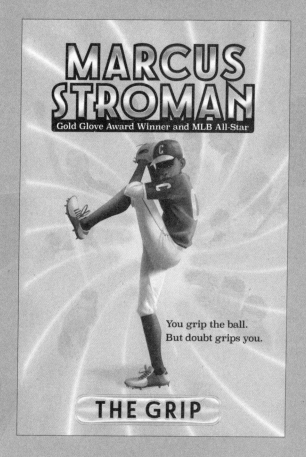

ABOUT THE AUTHOR

MARCUS STROMAN was born and raised in Medford, New York, where he attended Patchogue-Medford High School. Drafted by the Washington Nationals in the eighteenth round of the 2009 Major League Baseball draft, Marcus opted to delay the start of his professional career and chose to attend Duke University to further his education instead. He has pitched for the Toronto Blue Jays and the New York Mets and currently plays for the Chicago Cubs.

Marcus is passionate about his work with the community through his charitable HDMH (Height Doesn't Measure Heart) Foundation, where his work helps kids achieve their own dreams and instill confidence in themselves. While spreading his idea of believing in yourself more than believing in what anyone says about you, Marcus strives to be a positive role model both on and off the field.

Marcus has always believed in himself and has proven his critics wrong at every step of his journey. He is known for his determination in everything he does while building his confidence in whatever he sets out to do. He hopes to help kids build that same kind of confidence.